Readers love
RICK R. REED

The Couple Next Door

"I did have fun reading it… However, I will probably be sleeping with the lights on and probably will never date again after reading this."
—MM Good Book Reviews

"Of the several Rick R. Reed books I've had the pleasure to review, this one is the best."
—Inked Rainbow Reviews

Tricks

"Outstanding book. Highly recommended."
—On Top Down Under Reviews

"My breath was caught in my throat, my hands shook, and I couldn't sleep. I love and hate this story for that."
—Boys in Our Books

Dinner at Fiorello's

"This is the second book I've read from this author, and I was just as charmed as before with his characters and the lush setting descriptions."
—Joyfully Jay

"Reed has crafted a lovely and almost heartbreaking story about two men coping with loss."
—The Novel Approach

By RICK R. REED

Bashed
Big Love
Blink
Caregiver
Chaser • Raining Men
The Couple Next Door
Dignity Takes a Holiday
Dinner at Fiorello's
Dinner at Home
Homecoming
Hungry for Love
Husband Hunters
Legally Wed
Simmer (Dreamspinner Anthology)
Tricks

Published by DREAMSPINNER PRESS
www.dreamspinnerpress.com

BIG LOVE

RICK R. REED

Published by
DREAMSPINNER PRESS

5032 Capital Circle SW, Suite 2, PMB# 279, Tallahassee, FL 32305-7886 USA
www.dreamspinnerpress.com

Big Love
© 2016 Rick R. Reed.

Cover Art
© 2016 Reese Dante.
http://www.reesedante.com
Cover content is for illustrative purposes only and any person depicted on the cover is a model.

ISBN: 978-1-63476-976-1
Digital ISBN: 978-1-63476-977-8
Library of Congress Control Number: 2015920898
Published April 2016
v. 1.0

Printed in the United States of America
∞
This paper meets the requirements of
ANSI/NISO Z39.48-1992 (Permanence of Paper).

This book is dedicated to all the Trumans.

Acknowledgments

As always, I'd like to thank my Dreamspinner Press family for giving my stories such a welcoming home. And forever-gratitude to my husband, Bruce, who is my greatest supporter… and greatest love.

"I know I can't tell you what it's like to be gay. But I can tell you what it's not. It's not hiding behind words, Mama. Like family and decency and Christianity."
—*Armistead Maupin*

"Never be bullied into silence. Never allow yourself to be made a victim.

Accept no one's definition of your life; define yourself."
—*Harvey Fierstein*

"Every gay person must come out. As difficult as it is, you must tell your immediate family. You must tell your relatives. You must tell your friends if indeed they are your friends. You must tell the people you work with. You must tell the people in the stores you shop in. Once they realize that we are indeed their children, that we are indeed everywhere, every myth, every lie, every innuendo will be destroyed once and for all. And once you do, you will feel so much better."
—*Harvey Milk*

LATE AUGUST

PROLOGUE

DANE BERNARD, a big, gentle man, a teacher, would always look at that particular first day of school at Summitville High School as the one that changed his life forever.

Three things happened in that one momentous day that made returning to his old, comfortable life impossible—he rescued a boy from bullies, he lost his wife of twenty years, and... he began a journey to find himself.

How these three events, seemingly so disparate, tie together is our story. Let's begin with the first.

CHAPTER 1

TRUMAN REID was white as a stick of chalk—skin so pale it was nearly translucent. His blue eyes were fashioned from icy spring water. His hair—platinum blond—lay in curls across his forehead and spilled down his neck. He was the kind of boy for whom adjectives like "lovely" and "pretty" would most definitely apply. More than once in his life, he was mistaken for a girl.

When he was a very little boy, well-meaning strangers (and some not so well-meaning) would ask if he was a boy or a girl. Truman was never offended by the question, because he could see no shame in being mistaken for a girl. It wasn't until later that he realized there were some who would think the question offensive.

But this boy, who, on the first day of school, boldly and some might say unwisely wore a T-shirt that proclaimed "It Gets Better" beneath an image of a rainbow flag, didn't seem to possess the pride the T-shirt proclaimed. At Summitville High School, even though it was 2015, one did not shout out one's sexual orientation, not in word, not in fashion, and certainly not in deed.

Who knew what caused Truman to break with convention that morning when he made up his mind to wear that T-shirt on the first day of school? It wasn't like he needed to proclaim *anything*—after all, the slight, effeminate boy had been the object of bullies and torturers since, oh, about second grade. Truman could never "pass."

He was a big sissy. It was a fact and one Truman had no choice but to accept.

His shoulders, perpetually hunched, hunched farther during his grade school and junior high years, when such epithets as "sissy," "fag," "pansy," and "queer" were hurled at him in school corridors and playgrounds on a daily basis. Truman knew the old schoolyard chant wasn't true at all—words could and did hurt. And so, occasionally, did fists and hands.

4

And yet, despite the teasing—or maybe it's more apt to say *because* of it—Truman was not ashamed of who and what he was. His single mom, Patsy, his most vocal supporter and defender, often told him the same thing. "God made you just the way you are, honey. Beautiful. And if you're one of his creations, there's nothing wrong in who you are. You just hold your head up and be proud." The sad truth was, Patsy would often tell her boy stuff like this as she brushed tears away from his face.

It wasn't only tears she brushed away, though. Her unconditional love also brushed away any doubt Truman might have had that he was anything other than a normal boy, even though he was not like most of the boys his age in Summitville, Ohio, that backward little burg situated on the Ohio River and in the foothills of the Appalachian Mountains. In spite of the teasing and the bullying—and the pain they caused—Truman wasn't ashamed of who he was, which was what led him to wearing the fated T-shirt that got him in so much trouble his first day as a freshman at Summitville High School.

The incident occurred near the end of the day, when everyone was filing into the school gymnasium for an orientation assembly and a speech from the school's principal, Doug Calhoun, on what the returning students and incoming freshmen could expect that year.

Truman was in the crush of kids making their way toward the bleachers. High school was no different than grade school or junior high in that Truman was alone. And even though this was the first day of school, Truman already had a large three-ring binder tucked under his arm, along with English Composition, Biology, and Algebra I textbooks. Tucked into the notebook and books were papers—class schedules of assignments and the copious notes the studious Truman had already taken.

Kirk Samson, a senior and starting quarterback on the football team, knew the laughs he could get if he tripped this little fag in his pride-parade T-shirt, so he held back a little in the crowd, waiting for just the right moment to thrust out a leg in front of the unsuspecting Truman, whose eyes were cast down to the polished gymnasium floor.

Truman didn't see the quarterback's leg until it was too late, and he stumbled, going down hard on one knee. That sight was *not* the funniest thing the crowd had seen, although the pratfall garnered a roar of appreciative laughter at Truman's expense. But what was funnier was when Truman's notebook, books, and papers all flew out from under his arm, landing in a mess on the floor.

Kirk, watching from nearby with a smirk on his face, whispered two words to the kids passing by: "Kick 'em. Kick 'em."

And the kids complied, sending Truman's notes, schedules, and texts across the gym floor, as Truman, on his knees, struggled to gather everything up, even as more and more students got in on the fun of sending them farther and farther out of his reach.

Now, *that* was the funniest thing the crowd had seen.

Who knows how long the hilarity would have gone on if an authority figure had not intervened?

DANE BERNARD, English teacher, gentle giant, cross-country track coach, and indisputably one of the most well-liked teachers at the school, saw what was happening to Truman and rushed over. He only wished he could have been quicker to act—the boy's books and papers were now kicked out almost to the middle of the gym floor.

Dane knelt down by Truman, though, and helped him pick everything up as the kids behind, their laughter dying to a few isolated giggles, scrammed for their seats among the bleachers. It took a long time for the titters and whispering to die down.

Once the papers had been haphazardly gathered and even more haphazardly stuffed back inside notebook and textbooks, Dane put what he hoped was a calming hand on Truman's shoulder and gave it a little squeeze.

"You okay, son?" he asked.

The boy didn't have to respond. Dane frowned as he took in the tears standing in the boy's eyes. "What's your name?"

"Truman. Truman Reid." As befitting his name, the slight boy's voice came out reedy, a little high, still cracking, the bane of adolescent males since time immemorial.

"I'm Mr. Bernard."

Truman stared up at Dane, and as he did, a tear dribbled down his cheek, across a couple of acne bumps, to land on the floor. "Thanks. Thanks for helping me." Truman wiped away any remaining tears with the back of his hand. "I should get to my seat."

Dane looked over at the crowd, many of whom were watching, giggles ready to burst forth from their mean little faces. Dane thought there was no creature crueler on God's green earth than the teenage boy or girl. He squeezed Truman's shoulder. "Listen, the assembly's no biggie. Rules and regulations. Making sure you have 'an attitude that will determine your altitude.' Crap like that. You wanna skip it?" With a gentle smile, Dane tried to convey he cared. "We could go sit together someplace quiet for a bit and just chat." Dane shrugged. "No pressure."

"I don't know." The boy looked toward the crowd. Dane was disheartened when he followed his gaze. He didn't see one welcoming face.

"Come on," Dane said. "I've got Starburst in my homeroom."

"Well then, if you've got Starburst, how can I possibly say no?" And at last Truman smiled.

That smile was the kind of thing that made Dane get up every morning and come to work.

"Follow me."

Dane led the boy along the school corridor—green tile floors bracketed on either side by rows and rows of lockers in the same shade of industrial green. The boy, Truman, stopped at one of the lockers and began trying to work its combination lock. Dane paused to watch, figuring the boy wanted to divest himself of the load of books and papers he lugged around. Who had so much *stuff* on the first day of the semester?

Truman whispered what sounded like a curse to Dane as he did battle with the lock. He couldn't get it. He tried several times, spinning and spinning to no good effect. His books and papers once more tumbled to the floor. The situation was so sad, so pathetic, it almost made Dane want to laugh. Not at the boy, no, but at the absurdity of life and how it could simply be so plain cruel as to kick this harmless-looking boy when he was so down.

Dane didn't laugh. He neared Truman as the boy crumpled to the floor, sobbing.

Dane squatted next to him and patted his back. "It's okay. It's okay. Get your things together. We can get your combination from the janitor. No prob. Come on. Pick your stuff up and come back to my office."

Dane's heart just about broke as the boy looked up at him, cheeks damp and snot on his upper lip. What a way to start the year! He took in the shirt the boy was wearing and thought he might as well have affixed one of those "Kick Me" signs to his back before starting school this morning. *Why ask for trouble?* Dane wondered. Maybe he could figure the kid out once he got him to his office. Maybe he could let him know that some things that were personal should remain that way.

Truman stood, unsteady, a colt getting to its feet for the first time. He looked wildly around, like he was trapped there in the corridor. "I wanna go home," Truman said, voice barely above a whisper.

"Don't you wanna talk?" Dane asked, his eyebrows coming together with concern. "You'll find my homeroom is a judgment-free zone."

"I want to go home," Truman repeated, his voice a little louder.

"Do you walk to school?"

Truman shook his head.

"Buses won't be here for—" Dane glanced down at his watch, a Fossil timepiece with an orange band his wife, Katy, had gotten him last Christmas. "—another forty-five minutes. Come on. We'll wait in my homeroom." To repeat the offer of Starburst seemed like a silly incentive now. "Let's just go there and chill a little. You're a freshman, right?"

Truman nodded.

Dane grinned. "Come on. How many chances will you get to skip out on an assembly with a *teacher*? You like books?"

Truman nodded.

"Good. I teach English. You'd be surprised how many kids don't, how the only things they read are text messages, tweets, and status updates on Facebook. Who do you like to read?" Dane started walking toward his homeroom, hoping to coax Truman along.

8

"I like Stephen King and Dean Koontz," Truman said, not moving. "And I wanna go home."

"I like them too. I read my first King when I was about your age. *Christine*, I think it was. You read that one? About the possessed car? Sick!"

"Look, sir, you're being really nice and all, but I need to get home. I know the final bell hasn't rung yet, but do you think you could let me slide? I don't have to tell you I've had a rotten day, and I just need to get home, where I can hide."

Dane shook his head, not to refuse Truman's request but at the sadness of how the boy viewed home. "Where do you live?"

"Little England. It's only a mile or so from here."

Dane scratched his chin. Little England was one of the poorest neighborhoods in Summitville, bordered by the Ohio River on one side and railroad tracks on the other. The neighborhood, sitting just below river level, was regularly flooded. The houses there were mostly adorned with rusting aluminum siding. Or they were wooden frame in need of paint. Little England was poor. Dirty. And for Truman, Dane supposed, it was home.

"I can walk. Can you just look the other way? Please? Just for today?" Tears sprung up in Truman's eyes again. "I could use a break."

Dane so wanted to say yes, but there would be consequences if something should happen to the boy on his way home. Serious consequences, the kind where he could lose his job. And with twenty years here at the school, two kids and a wife to support, he couldn't let that happen. Yet the terror and pain on this boy's face rent his heart in two. "Tell you what," Dane said finally. "If you can call someone to come get you—your mom or your dad—I can let you go with them. Otherwise—" Dane stopped himself as he watched Truman pull a phone out of his pocket. His fingers flew over the tiny screen. Dane was amazed how even the poorest of kids these days managed to have cell phones.

Truman didn't look at him. Instead he stared at the screen as if willing it to life. After a minute or so, Truman breathed a sigh of relief. He held the screen of the flip phone up so Dane could see. Dane read the shorthand texts, which basically confirmed that Mom could get off from work and pick him up in ten minutes, but she wanted to know what was wrong.

What *wasn't* wrong? Dane imagined Truman thinking.

"Can I go wait outside?" Truman asked.

Dane sighed. "Sure you don't want to come talk to me? Just for a few minutes? We'll see your mom pull up from my window."

"You just have to make this as hard as you can, don't you?" Truman snapped.

Dane's smile faltered. "I was trying to do just the opposite," he said.

Truman's face reddened. "I'm sorry, man. I just need to get home."

Dane nodded. "I get it. Go ahead. Wait outside for your mom."

Truman started away, walking quickly, books still stuffed under one matchstick arm.

Dane called after him, "Come talk to me tomorrow. We'll get your locker combination figured out." *Among other things*, Dane thought as he turned to head back to his homeroom.

Once there, Dane plopped down in his imitation-leather desk chair and sighed. He rubbed his hands over his face. Seeing kids teased and bullied was, unfortunately, part of the job, and over two decades, Dane had lost count of the number of times he had witnessed cruelty. Sometimes he thought high school students had cornered the market on unkindness.

But Truman Reid bothered him more than most. It was that damn T-shirt he wore, one that might as well have proclaimed "I'm a big old fag" on the front, instead of its message of hope and the pride of the rainbow flag. Kids here just looked for any excuse to tease, to belittle. The jocks especially seemed to feel that someone's being gay was as good a reason as any to make their life a living hell.

Dane was just about to reflect on the relevance being gay had on his own life when his phone rang. For a moment he was grateful for the ringtone, because it saved him from some of his darkest ruminations, thoughts he shared with no one, but which Truman—with his damnable and enviable pride—had brought out in him.

He pulled his iPhone from his pocket and glanced down at the screen. Unknown, Caller ID taunted him. Dane was tempted not to answer, to just let it go to voice mail and head for the student assembly so he could at least say he'd been there, but instead he pressed Accept.

"Dane Bernard here." He fully expected a telemarketer.

"Mr. Bernard." A male voice came over the line. "Is this the husband of Katherine Bernard?"

A chill coursed through him. "Yup." He tried to swallow, but the sudden dryness in his mouth nearly prevented it. "Is everything all right?"

"I'm sorry to tell you this, Mr. Bernard, but there's been an accident involving your wife. This is Bill Rogers, by the way, with the State Highway Patrol."

Dane could feel his whole body go cold, as if dipped in ice water. "But she's okay, right?" he managed to gasp.

The man responded, "Do you think you could come down to City Hospital? I'll meet you at the ER. Just ask for Bill Rogers. I'll wait."

"Is she okay?" Dane repeated, gripping the phone—hard. But the patrolman had already hung up.

CHAPTER 2

TRUMAN HELD his hand up to his eyes to shield them from the sun as he watched for his mother's car—a rusting Dodge Neon that was older than he was. Patsy called it "Herman," although Truman had no idea why. Truman would hear its grumbling muffler before he actually saw the car. But right now, seeing the car was the most welcome sight Truman could imagine.

He tried to hold it together, the tears and the sobs inside threatening to break free like an itch needing to be scratched.

He closed his eyes with a kind of relief as he saw the little gray car coming down the street, a plume of exhaust belching out of its back end. The car swung rapidly to the curb, front wheels going up on it, and screeched to a stop right in front of Truman.

He was used to his mother's driving. He rushed to get in the car, ignoring the whine it made when he opened the passenger door.

His mother sat across from him, looking glamorous as always. Today Patsy had on dark jeans, a blue lace crop top, and strappy rhinestone sandals that matched her dangling earrings. Her dyed black hair hung in loose curls to her shoulders. Truman thought she could waltz right into the school and fit in perfectly with the other teenage girls—no problem—even though Patsy was the ripe old age of thirty-one.

All his life, it had just been the two of them against the world. Truman didn't know who his father was and, in darker moments, figured Patsy didn't either. She took her hand off the shifter and looked over with concern.

"What happened? What's wrong?"

Truman had never been able to keep a secret from Patsy. He sniffed once and said, "How'd you know?"

She touched his cheek, which had the paradoxical effect of making Truman want both to flinch and to bask in the warmth and comfort of her hand.

"Honey, that sad face is lower than a snake's belly."

"We were at an assembly, and I dropped my books and paper, and—" He could barely go on, getting his humiliation out in fits and starts between gasps for breath. He lowered his head and released the real sobs he'd been holding in since the kids had been so mean to him in the gym. His shoulders shook. His eyes burned. His nose ran. He felt like a baby, and at the same time experienced relief at finally letting his grief go. The worst part, he thought, was that jock who had tripped him telling everyone over and over to kick his stuff. And they all did what he said. And thought it was hysterical!

Patsy had the sense to drive away from the school as Truman sobbed into his hands. He felt like there was a tennis ball in his throat. He just wanted to get home, where he could curl up in bed with his dog at his side. The dog, a mix of bulldog and dachshund that everyone but Truman thought was hideous, was named Odd Thomas, or Odd for short, after a character from a series of Dean Koontz books that Truman adored. The name, though, fit the mutt.

Patsy also had the sense not to say a word until they pulled up in front of their house, a little two-bedroom cottage sided with some kind of tarpaper that was supposed to look like brick but just looked like shit. The front porch appeared as though it could fall off at any time. But Truman never complained—he knew Patsy was providing the best home she could for the two of them on her waitress's salary and tips.

She put a gentle hand on his shoulder that felt as good as a hug.

Truman, able to speak at last, said, "And don't say I shouldn't have worn this shirt to school! You bought it for me!"

"I wasn't gonna say that, sweetie. I think it's a cute shirt, and you have every right to wear it."

Truman should have known. His mother had found the shirt at Goodwill last month. Truman had thought how lucky he was to have a mom like Patsy when she brought it home to him. It was a kind of tribute to Patsy that he had worn it today. He knew he'd probably catch shit for it, but as Patsy always told him, there was no shame in being who he was. If someone had a problem with it, the problem was theirs, not his.

It all sounded good when they were curled up in front of the TV watching *Grey's Anatomy* together or something, but in the real world? Truman was not only gay, he was a very sensitive boy whose feelings were easily crushed. What was he supposed to do with that?

"Come on. I brought home some fries and gravy from the diner, and if they get too cold, they're gonna taste like crap." Patsy got out of the car and waited for him to follow.

Truman wanted to simply dash from the car and hole up in his room with Odd, but he knew Patsy wouldn't leave him alone. He loved her and hated her for it.

So he shuffled in behind his mother, snuffling and rubbing at his burning eyes. Odd jumped off the couch and ran up to him. Truman stooped and let the dog lick his face hungrily. Truman wasn't kidding himself—he knew the dog's extra kisses weren't meant to be a sign of joy at his homecoming or a comfort, but simply a way to taste the saltiness that was so delicious on Truman's skin.

Truman endured the facial tongue bath for several seconds, then scratched Odd behind the ear and patted him on the head.

"I'll go in and heat these up and make us some burgers while you run him out, okay?" Patsy smiled and nodded toward the leash hanging on a hook by the door.

Truman set his school stuff down on the table and headed out with the dog.

"Don't be long," Patsy called after him.

Outside, it still felt like summer. The quality of light, so bright, promised forever day. The breezes were still warm. And those clouds, puffy cotton-ball affairs, seemed painted on the bright blue sky. Insect life hummed as a soundtrack.

Odd urged him on, down toward the banks of the Ohio River where he was happiest. Truman was happy there too. The river was muddy brown and smelled fishy, but the low-hanging trees, willows and maples mostly, shielded Truman from the world, made him feel blissfully alone. And alone was not such a bad thing to be when the world seemed to take every opportunity to kick him in the teeth.

Truman released Odd from his leash and let him run on the riverbank, sniffing at the detritus the river had thrown up. There were old tires, tree branches, cans, and other stuff so worn down by the water it was impossible to identify. Truman sat down on a log while the dog splashed at the water's edge.

Maybe Patsy would say he could just stay home from high school. Was fourteen too young to drop out? Or—wait—maybe she could homeschool him? Right! Like she had extra hours on her hands for that.

Truman stood and skipped a rock across the water's surface, wondering how it would feel to just walk into the brown current until it swallowed him up and carried him away, erasing all his woes. He imagined the cool green surrounding him, his blond hair flowing in the current, those last final bubbles from his nose and mouth ascending toward the sunlight above the water....

But then he thought of his mother. He could imagine her grief, her utter devastation if he was gone. She'd be alone. He couldn't do that to her.

He sighed.

He trudged home, knowing what Patsy would say—how he had to be strong, how he had to be proud of who he was and not take shit from anyone. He'd heard the same speech a thousand times over the course of his short and sissified life. It was cool that his mom was so in his corner, that she was so accepting, but sometimes Truman just wished he wasn't one of the misfit toys, that he was just a normal boy, playing Little League or whatever it was that normal boys did. One of the guys. His mother would tell him that what he wished for was to be common, to be unremarkable, and that someday he'd be glad he was different. It was easy for her to say, or at least so he thought, since she was beautiful, and the worst she had to deal with was being hit on by the truckers and traveling salesmen who came into the diner.

As he neared the porch, he called for Odd to come and, when he did, squatted down to reattach the leash to his collar. Patsy didn't allow the dog to roam free outside. She said it was because she was afraid he'd run away.

Truman wondered if it was really Odd Thomas she feared running away.

He turned and faced the house. Through the screen door, he could hear and smell the ground beef sizzling in its cast-iron skillet and could smell the brown gravy as it surely bubbled on the stove, and the aromas made him, surprisingly, hungry.

Home was a good place.

And tomorrow was another day. Maybe things would be different.

"Yeah, right," he whispered to Odd as he followed him through the door.

CHAPTER 3

BILL ROGERS, state highway patrolman, was gone. Dane sat alone in the City Hospital waiting room, feeling stung, Rogers's words echoing in his brain like some mantra: "dead at the scene, dead at the scene." Dane laughed, bitter, and thought the words should be set to music. Rogers had tried—not too hard because it wasn't working—to comfort him by saying that when that drunk driver had swerved into Katy, causing her SUV to flip, that she was "killed instantly." It was like his wife had won the death lottery, the best way to go. Killed instantly. Woo-hoo.

How did Bill Rogers know, anyway? How did he know she didn't feel terror, loss, and pain in mere seconds as her life rushed out of her like water swirling around a drain, faster and faster? No one knew, or could ever know, what Katy's final moments might have been like. Had her life flashed before her eyes? Had she been happy with what she saw? Had she felt loved?

Was she now in some dark but warm corridor that Dane imagined as the interior of a softly beating heart, moving toward a welcoming light where she knew loved ones who had passed on before waited with open minds, hearts, and arms? Or was she hovering above this very waiting room, watching Dane as he waited for his kids to arrive?

Did she, watching, at last see her husband for who he really was? Did she finally see his secrets? Did death give her the capacity to still love him despite what she saw? Did she understand why he'd worn a mask all these years? Did she know, in her stilled heart, that in spite of everything, Dane had really loved her? That he had no regrets?

Or if she was here, floating somewhere near the ceiling, was she disappointed in what she saw in her husband?

Dane felt guilty he wasn't a wreck. He wanted to pinch himself hard to perhaps start the flow of tears he knew he should be crying.

Yet for all the stinging numbness within him—and there was a wall of it, rising—he couldn't manage a single tear.

He felt, pardon the expression, dead. He wondered if he was in shock. It would make sense, wouldn't it? When he got up that morning, preparing to head back to the school where he taught after the summer off, the world was normal. Now it had been spun around, turned upside down, changed so completely that nothing would ever be the same again.

This numbness, this lack of emotion, felt weird, like an alien presence had invaded his body and mind. As the minutes ticked by, Dane would remind himself where he was and what had happened. He would forget for whole minutes, staring, blinking at the sterile waiting room, uncomprehending. He would have to pull his location up in his head—City Hospital—and would have to grope for the reason he was there. Had he hurt himself? When a cursory check of his own body showed no wounds, the truth and the reason he was there would all rush back—cruelly.

His sport coat, the blue-and-black-checked one that looked so good with jeans, was on the chair beside him. Dane would stare at it in his worst moments, wondering to whom it belonged.

He tried to bring himself to the present, to feel *something* by remembering his last moments with Katy, that morning in their kitchen. She had made him a lunch—Tupperware filled with tomatoes and green onions from her garden, some feta cheese, olive oil, and a little red wine vinegar. To this she had added one of those pouches of tuna and a Granny Smith apple. Everything was packed neatly into a brown paper bag.

Dane had looked through it, rummaging through the bag, and then up at her, peering suspiciously into her brown eyes. "What is this? No chips? No little Hostess cupcake?" He cocked his head. "Are you saying I need to lose weight?"

In response she had patted his gut, which they both knew had been expanding little by little over the past decade, but Katy was too kind to tell Dane he was getting a bit of a beer belly. "Of course not, sweetie. I just think we need to eat healthier." She had pressed the bag in, toward his chest. "You take this. I made the same for Clarissa and Joey too."

"They'll never eat it. Joey will want to get a cheeseburger in the cafeteria, and Clarissa will probably have, oh, I don't know, a bottled water, and maybe a Tic Tac if she's really famished."

Katy shrugged, sat down at the table, and sipped her coffee. "All I can do is try with you guys."

"Well, thanks, babe. But I think I'll pass." He'd left the lunch on the kitchen table, and the last thing he did, he remembered now, was to kiss her—not on the lips, but on the top of her head, as though she were a child rather than a wife. And the last thing he said to the woman who would be dead only a few hours later? He had looked down at the part in her auburn hair and remarked, "You need to touch up these roots. I can see gray."

She had slapped his butt and told him to be on his way. "And take the lunch I made for you with you!"

But he hadn't. And the image of the little brown paper bag sitting on the kitchen table was what finally caused him to lower his head and let out an anguished cry. Why hadn't he taken it? Why hadn't he said something *nice* to her? Why hadn't he thanked her? Why hadn't he given her a proper kiss?

He covered his face with his hands and wept, the tears coming at last like some sort of emotional tsunami. He had wanted the tears to be there when the ER doctor had spoken to him, saying words like fractured this, internal bleeding, ruptured that. Dane had tuned the doctor out. It. Was. Not. Real. He had wanted to weep when a nurse came by, in pink scrubs with a smock imprinted with balloons, to try to offer him comfort. But he didn't need it then. He felt embarrassed and ashamed of his dry eyes and his bearing, which radiated the fact that he was doing A-OK.

What did it matter, anyway, who witnessed his grief? What did it matter that an image of a brown paper bag, stained a bit darker at the bottom with a little olive oil, abandoned on a kitchen table, just about tore his heart in two?

The only people he really cared about seeing him in this pitiable state were his children. For them he needed to be strong.

But it was too late. He heard Clarissa's voice before he saw her.

"Dad?" She sounded scared. "Dad? What's going on?"

And when he looked up, through his tear-blurred vision, he saw his baby girl and his little man. They'd taken two of the plastic seats on either side of him. He'd been crying so hard he hadn't even heard them come in. He looked over Joey's shoulder and saw a woman had also crept into the waiting room just behind his children. She was no one he knew, simply an old woman in a summer housedress, one his mom called a shift, sensible shoes, gray hair, and a handbag balanced on her knees beneath her folded, careworn hands. He wanted to ask her if she was here for her husband. Was it serious? Would he be all right? Did she spend much time in rooms like this?

He wanted to do anything except talk to his children. To do so would cement this moment in their young lives as one they would never forget, and not for a good reason. This wasn't supposed to happen. Yeah, the natural order of things had parents dying first. But not like this, not when there was a young girl just trying on what it felt like to be a woman. Not when there was a kid who was just leaving being a little boy behind yet still, damn it, needed his mother once in a while to tuck him in at night. Parents mostly *did* die first, but in Dane's mind it was when they were old and gray, when they had held a grandbaby in their arms and looked up with pride and tears at the child who had carried on with the family legacy.

No one should lose a mother this young, Dane thought. It just wasn't right.

He looked at Clarissa, who had the same auburn hair and brown eyes as her mother. Sixteen going on thirty, too thin for her own good but always looking in the mirror for errant fat, for a need to diet more and eat less. Now there was expectancy in those dark eyes, the anticipation of something heavy about to be lowered, the agony of waiting for something awful to come. Clarissa was like he had been when he had driven over here after getting the state highway patrolman's call—wishing, hoping, praying for an alternate reality, a world where things were bad, yes, of course, but not *too bad*. Now, in this space between waiting and the big truth, there was safety, there was *hope*. How could Dane take that away?

20

He turned his head to look at his son. He was only twelve! That was far too tender an age for a boy to lose his mother! What would he do without her? Could Dane fill her shoes, even in small ways? Joey stared straight ahead, once in a while gnawing at a hangnail on the edge of his thumb. Joey looked more like Dane, big, raw-boned, already over six feet, towering over his classmates. His hair was coarse, the color of straw, his eyes the dark blue of a newborn. Despite his size, there was such innocence to that face. Joey's jawline and nose, which Dane knew from his own countenance would one day be strong, angularly defined, were now softer, waiting for time to shape them.

He didn't want to take that innocence away prematurely.

How to break it to them?

Clarissa, unwittingly, urged him on.

"Dad? Dad, what's going on? Some cop picked us up at the bus stop outside of school and brought us here. He wouldn't tell us anything. What's happening? Is it Mom? Is she okay?"

With every word, every searching gaze, Clarissa said the same thing—*lie to me*. She knew as well as Dane had, driving to the hospital, that the game was over, the final bell had rung, but accepting that was another step, another progression in a journey neither her feet nor her mind and heart wanted to take.

Dane got it.

He grabbed Clarissa's hand, clutched it tight, and swiveled to look at Joey, who wouldn't look back but continued to simply stare ahead. Dane turned back to Clarissa and drew in a shuddering breath, wiping away tears he was just now aware dampened his face. He tried to sit up straighter.

He couldn't say the words. Later he would think that what his tortured psyche allowed him to say was worse than uttering the simple truth. "She'll want something simple."

"What?" Clarissa asked.

"She'll want it simple. Her funeral. Wildflowers and, uh, some classical music, something not sad. Bach? I don't know!" He snorted. "What do I know about classical? I used to think Billy Joel was high class."

"Dad?" Clarissa looked at him, blinking, her expression slack, expectant.

He reached out, desperately stroked her masses of reddish hair, his hand getting tangled up in it. He was trapped. He let his hand hang in her hair, feeling stupid. "She's gone, honey." He looked to Joey, who at last stared back. His eyes were filled with tears yet to spill.

To Joey he said, in an emotionless whisper, as official as that patrolman, "Your mother was killed in an accident involving a drunk driver this afternoon. When paramedics arrived, she was already gone." He turned back to Clarissa, managing to finally free his hand from her hair but clutching her with his other hand so hard that, when he looked down at their hands, they had both gone white, bloodless. "They said she was 'dead at the scene' and that—" His voice broke; he couldn't help it. A sob escaped like a hiccup. "And that she didn't suffer." He said the words he'd thought so foolish and futile earlier. "She was, um, *taken* instantly." He repeated, as much for his kids as for himself, "She didn't feel any pain."

And his kids, God bless them, became the parents for just a little while. Both Clarissa and Joey, as if born to it, knew to gather around their father. They knelt in front of him and at his side and wrapped their arms around him, holding him as he sobbed.

They cried too. There were no admonishments—wisely—from either child, telling him things would be okay (they wouldn't, no, not ever) or that they would get through this together. None of them knew at this point, Dane thought, how the broken path of their lives would affect their futures as they moved forward uncertainly with grief and rage as their companions.

It seemed like they were frozen in this little fractured family tableau for much longer than the time that actually passed, which had to have been only a few minutes at most. But in that moment where time stood still, Dane felt both joy, horror, and shame. Joy because he had these children, these products of his and his Katy's love, and it was more consolation, he thought, than he deserved.

The horror and shame came from the crashing and crushing realization that, with Katy gone, his secret self could finally emerge.

He could lay down the shield and the sword, cast off the mask. And the thought of doing that terrified him.

He eased away from his daughter's and son's caresses and stood. "Come on. We need to get home. There are a lot of things to be done. Calls to make. Arrangements."

He started from the waiting room, expecting Clarissa and Joey to follow, but they didn't. He looked back to see two lumps in orange plastic chairs. Wet faces and open mouths, trying to breathe.

"Come on," Dane urged gently.

Joey at last spoke, his voice a quiver, five years old again. "Are we just gonna leave Mommy here?" His voice went up, breaking on the word "Mommy." He seemed panicked. "We can't just leave her," he whispered.

Dane walked back, knelt before his son. He brushed hair off his forehead, digging deep for some vestige of strength he must have somewhere—he had to—and said, "We're not leaving her here." Dane let his hand slide down to the boy's cheek. "Because she's not here. What's here is a shell. You know? Your mom went to heaven when that car ran into her." Dane, at this moment, wasn't sure what he believed in as far as an afterlife. But he did believe that Joey was not too old for fairy tales, and if the idea of heaven was a small comfort to the boy, by God, he would believe in it, if only for the immediate present. "She's in heaven, Joey. What will stay here is kind of like a husk." He let his hand drop to his son's sweaty hand and squeezed. "She's with us right now, and she always will be. You can bet she's looking down on us, expecting us to do the right thing. Do right by her." He tugged at the boy's hand. "Come on now. Let's go home."

Clarissa was standing now, and she neared them. "It's what she would have wanted, Joey."

Dane stood too, and his eyes met his daughter's in a kind of understanding. She had grown up a lot in these last few moments.

Dane drew both of his kids close, his arms draped over their shoulders as they headed toward the green Exit sign, toward a future that was as terrifying as it was uncertain.

23

Dane paused as they reached the corridor that would lead them outside and felt as Joey had—they were just leaving her there?

How could they? How could he?

He drew in a breath, shut his eyes, and thought of his wife as she was as a young girl, a teenager at Ohio State University. She was in front of a bulletin board in her dorm, and she was smiling at him as if she already knew him, already knew the future they would share, and asked, "You're Dane, right?"

EARLY JANUARY

CHAPTER 4

SETH WOLCOTT sat in his Nissan Leaf electric car in the parking lot of Summitville High School, watching everyone go inside. They were all hurrying, heads bent, because the snow was coming down faster and faster. When he had started up the Leaf, the snow was little more than a few flakes, dancing on the currents of freezing air—pretty.

Now it was a threat. Surely this first day of school after the holiday break would have been canceled if they could have seen what was poised on the brink. Now the snow drifted down so hard, it was accumulating fast and blotting out the hill-covered landscape under a screen of white.

Seth could use the day off, even if it was his first at the school, sliding into a spot as an English teacher—with a specialty in drama—that had been vacated last semester by Gretchen Schmidbauer, who'd gone on maternity leave when she gave birth, like the Virgin Mary, on Christmas Eve. Seth could only hope she'd had her little one in a hospital, rather than a barn, because Summitville was fucking *cold*.

Not that it was any better where he'd just been—the Windy City, the Second City, the place Carl Sandburg had called the City of Big Shoulders. Chicago. The place where Seth had lived his entire adult life, or at least since he had set out for parts west, not getting very far after graduating from Indiana University at the early part of the new millennium. Sandburg, in that same poem where he christened the city, also called Chicago "brutal." And Seth had to snort at that, because although he agreed with the poet's assessment, he was certain Mr. Sandburg had a completely different opinion on what constituted "brutal" from Seth's.

A quick image flashed in his mind—his boyfriend, no, fiancé, Luke, and his surprised face, over broad naked shoulders, when Seth came home early from teaching English at Senn High School. He had found Luke on the couch with his legs in the air, his buddy Ryan, from the gym, between them.

Seth snorted with bitter laughter. He'd thought, until that morning, when the beginnings of the flu had sent him home after lunch, that such tawdry antics only occurred in the movies, to people like Sandra Bullock. It was a cheap plot point. It didn't really happen to people, not in real life.

It wasn't so romantic comedy when it happened to you.

"But it was only the one time!" Luke had tried to assure him later, as if that made a difference, as if that would make Seth feel better. One time or a hundred, the betrayal still stung like hell. Their trust had been ruined. Seth hadn't realized how important—and fragile—trust could be until he'd lost it.

Seth hastily canceled their Christmas nuptials and was lucky to find the job in eastern Ohio right away. He'd never heard of Summitville, but oblivion and escape was what he craved. The picture on Wikipedia of the little Ohio town on the river, in its valley of tree-covered hills, looked like a place where Seth could vanish.

The snow, as suddenly as it had made a blizzard, seemed to change its mind and head in the opposite direction. Seth looked up at the dwindling flakes, now sparkling with early morning sun, and saw a patch of blue had opened up among the heavy gray clouds.

Maybe it was an omen. Perhaps a chorus of angelic voices should have sounded with the appearance of that patch of blue. Maybe the universe was telling him that this new beginning, in a place where he knew absolutely no one, had been the right choice. He whispered to himself, "Yeah, right, the universe, so vast and mysterious, so chaotic, has made *my* happiness its business. And is sending me signs to boot!"

Seth gathered up his messenger bag from the passenger seat to go inside and stopped when a man passing his car caught his eye. Seth's breath froze in his mouth. If he'd been asked, even seconds ago, if any man could "catch his eye" in his current state of loss and betrayal, Seth would have said "Get out of here!" and meant it.

But the libido and the roving eye of a relatively young man were not as unforgiving as the heart. Eye and libido still had their needs despite a smashed heart, Seth thought, staring at the stranger in the navy blue coat as he passed by Seth's Leaf. Seth took in the broad shoulders, the proud bearing, and the shaved head that said, in no uncertain terms, that a real *man* was passing by.

Seth was surprised at the pulse of longing and electricity that coursed through him at just a glimpse of this stranger, who must also be on the faculty, because Seth would have judged him at least a few years older than himself.

And he was gorgeous! First, it was just his sheer size, his magnitude that caused Seth's pulse to quicken. Seth liked 'em big, he always had, and this guy was a giant. He must have been around six feet six inches and was, as they said in the ads, HWP, or height and weight proportionate. What? Two hundred? Two twenty? No matter. Seth's fickle lust could only imagine what all that height and weight would feel like spread out on top of him. A man blanket. The mind reeled.

Shame on you, Seth Wolcott! his conscious mind admonished in the voice of Dana Carvey's Church Lady. In that same superego-inspired voice, Seth asked, *"What's gotten into you? Satan?"* And he answered, ignoring the reference to Satan, *"I don't know, but I know what I'd like to get into me."*

Seth shook his head and permitted his sad-sack self an indulgent grin. He pulled his messenger bag on his lap to both get himself going and to hide the burgeoning erection in his jeans. Just as he was about to open the door, the giant turned his head to look at a colleague coming up the front walk, and it was his face that really sealed the deal. That face, so angular, so manly, so *kind*, caused Cupid to release his arrow from its bow. "It's hopeless!" Seth wailed. "I haven't even gotten out of the car yet on my very first day, and already my heart has been stolen." His erection, growing ever harder, reminded him that, in all actuality, another organ was the object of thievery.

But the guy *was* beautiful, the kind of man Seth's fantasies would conjure up and file under the word *perfection*. Seth admonished himself in a whispering voice, hoping no one saw his lips moving, "He's probably the wrestling—or no, the football—coach and is as straight as they come. Let's not sentence ourselves to unrequited pining on our first day! Get out of the fuckin' car and be a professional, not one of those adolescent boys you are about to teach—ones whose hormones are in overdrive."

The wind, despite the snow dribbling down to a few spotty flakes, was bitter when Seth opened his door. He watched as his giant went inside the school and wondered if he'd have the chance to meet him today. Seth hurried up the walk. He had an appointment with the principal, Doug Calhoun, first thing, and he didn't want to be late.

Just as he neared the door, the giant turned, as if he felt Seth's rapt gaze upon him. Or maybe he had—what was the word?—a *presentiment* that Seth was about to do something righteously embarrassing and hysterical.

And perhaps because Seth worried about making an ass out of himself in front of this man he found gorgeous, he did precisely that. The universe, once again laser-focused on Seth, caused his right foot to come down on a patch of ice cunningly hidden in a shadow cast by Summitville High. His foot went dramatically forward, extending so much it called to Seth's mind an old Monty Python sketch, "The Ministry of Silly Walks." Right leg extended beyond what was natural, Seth crumpled to one knee, a silly grin barely masking his pain. He tried to grab his messenger bag to keep it off the wet ground and succeeded in somehow flipping his body down so that he did a cheek plant on the asphalt. His glasses skittered across yet another unseen patch of ice.

He lay on the ground gasping, wishing that blizzard-like snow would return and mercifully bury him. Wasn't there some way he could just make himself melt into the ground, a la the Wicked Witch of the West?

Alas, real life did not offer him any such flights of fancy. Seth felt a strong pair of hands on his shoulders, gently pulling him up. He didn't have to look to know whose they were. And as much as he wanted to meet this man he'd just rhapsodized over in the car, he was now recalling the old adage, "Be careful what you wish for." He didn't care. He wished again—wished that he'd look up and someone else would come to his aid. Perhaps a nice middle-aged algebra teacher, the water polo team coach, perhaps? Or maybe a student who wanted to brownnose the new teacher.

Of course, the universe could have none of that. It was none other than the object of Seth's lust tugging him kindly upright again. Seth looked into his eyes—blue as that patch of sky he'd seen emerge earlier—and tried to smile, but it was damned hard to do when his face was burning so fiercely Seth was surprised it didn't melt the snow for miles around.

"Are you okay?"

Seth struggled to get to his feet, grunting, awkward, and his hunky Good Samaritan rose with him. Seth stooped once more to snatch his glasses from the ground, thankful they weren't broken or thrown out of alignment. He clumsily affixed the horn-rims to his face and met the gaze of the man before him. "Okay? Other than feeling like a complete jackass, I'm swell. Right as rain." Seth attempted a grin but had a feeling it came out more as a grimace.

The guy cocked his head, looking at Seth like he was some sort of curious specimen.

"I'm Dane Bernard," he said. "I teach English here. And you are?"

"You're Dane Bernard?" Seth asked, laughing. "I'm supposed to meet with you this morning. You're going to be what they call my faculty buddy." Seth's mind went to another f-word buddy he wouldn't mind Dane being. And what a great name! Dane! It seemed so, so—big—and strong and manly. *Great Dane!*

Seth mentally kicked himself. He was thinking like a schoolgirl, if what was running through his head could be properly qualified as thinking at all. And regardless of his very close proximity to a school, schoolgirl or even schoolboy thought was simply not acceptable. He wiped the grit off his hands on his jeans and extended one of them to Dane. "Seth Wolcott."

Dane's features relaxed into a smile. "You're Gretchen's replacement. Principal Calhoun has told me all about you. Chicago, huh?" Dane clapped a hand on his shoulder. "Buddy, you're in a different world now."

Seth wondered if Dane was privy to the sordid details of why he'd fled Chicago, heart roadburned by infidelity. He doubted it. *Somehow,* Seth chastised himself, *you need to pull yourself together.*

He took a deep breath and allowed himself the time to let it out slowly. "Right. Right! I'm so happy to be here! So happy, in fact, I tried to dance a little jig, but I kind of screwed that up." He chuckled.

Dane smiled, and his expression reflected the two-word thought he suspected was running through Dane's mind at that moment—*humor him.*

"Uh-huh," Dane said, just as the final bell rang. He looked Seth up and down. "If you're sure you're okay, no broken bones, no concussions or cracked ribs, I need to get inside. My homeroom can get out of hand quicker than you could imagine."

"Oh, I could imagine. I taught at an inner-city high school in Chicago."

"I'm sure this will be a little different. Good luck. We'll talk later, okay?" And without waiting for a response, Dane Bernard turned and hurried inside the school, along with a few final straggling students.

Seth started up the steps, when he felt a tap on his shoulder. He turned to see a woman about his own age, with red hair styled in a kind of retro 1960s bubble cut. She was grinning. Her green eyes seemed magnified by her Catwoman glasses. She wore a coat that had to have come from the Salvation Army store or a very fancy vintage clothing store—teal, knee-length, wool, with big plastic buttons. Everything about her screamed "character," and Seth immediately drew the conclusion that was entirely her goal.

"Be careful with that one."

"Oh?"

"Yeah," she said in a kind of motherly, pitying tone, leaning in close.

How she managed to put all that into one word was beyond Seth, but she did it.

"He just lost his wife." She lowered her voice to a whisper. "Car accident."

"Oh, that's too bad." Seth wanted to slap himself for having the thought that a wife—even a dead one—probably equaled Dane Bernard being as straight as a two-by-four. "And you are?"

32

"Betsy. Wagner. Human Sexuality 101 and health sciences."

She held out a white-mittened hand, and Seth took it, squeezing gratefully.

"I'll take you to the principal's office, mister," she said sternly and then laughed.

"Seth Wolcott. English composition, Introduction to Poetry, and Drama."

Betsy said, "I know who you are. Everybody does."

"Oh really?"

"Yeah. No secrets at Summitville High."

Seth rolled his eyes as he followed her into the Gothic-styled redbrick building. He cast a quick glance behind him. The snow was coming down harder again. He longed to go back out into it, to lose himself in a curtain of white. He wondered if he had made the right choice.

CHAPTER 5

DANE WATCHED the gaggle of laughing, shoving, and gossiping college preparatory literature students move almost as one hormone-fueled beast out of his classroom. It was the end of third period, and Dane was glad. End of third period signaled the beginning of Dane's free period for lesson planning, and for that he was grateful.

He didn't need to lesson plan. He needed a breather. He needed to think.

The class was a new specialty literature course for advanced kids, and it was one Dane had petitioned for and one for which he had come up with the syllabus. "Adolescent Angst and the Antihero" sounded more like a class most of these kids would take in college, and that had been Dane's plan—to introduce some of the more advanced students to college-level thinking about literature and how it shaped human thought.

But the first book he had chosen, one he'd had to fight to include, now stuck out to him as fateful, or synchronous to his own life, even though he didn't think the parallels would be apparent to anyone other than himself.

The book was Alice Sebold's *The Lovely Bones*, and it told the story of Susie Salmon, a teenage girl who is raped and murdered in the first few pages of the book. For the remainder of the story, Susie watches over her family, friends, and even her killer from heaven. "It's a story about loss. It's a story about discovery... and moving on. It's a story, in the end, about *life*," Dane had told the class, thinking he was merely trying to instill an interest in the novel's themes over its more lurid opening sequence of events.

But his subconscious was busy working in the background. And that's why Dane now found himself sitting at his desk with the lights off, watching the snow come down outside. It had settled into a gentle fall, the flakes big and fluffy—pretty. Most of the stuff wasn't even sticking. Rather, it danced across the sidewalk in front of the school like lint escaped from a dryer.

Dane, of course, hadn't lost his own life like Susie Salmon. But he had experienced loss, and even though he was still breathing, still eating, still sleeping at night, even though his nights were sometimes interrupted by nightmares and bad memories, he was alive.

Yet the life he had known, back at the beginning of the school year, was gone, snuffed out just as surely as that drunk driver had snuffed out Katy's life on that highway.

He had worn his grief, over the rest of the past semester, like something heavy and chained around his neck, moving through life in a daze, simply going through the motions. Thank God Clarissa and Joey helped keep things on track for their sad-sack father! Those kids, he sometimes thought, were more resilient than he was. Shouldn't it have been the other way around?

But now, with the start of a new year and a new semester, Dane was determined to be a real parent to his kids again.

And he was determined about something else too. It was *The Lovely Bones* that helped bring out that determination, or at least solidify it. In the book, the character comes to see her helplessness at changing anything in the lives of the people she loves. Even though she knows everything about her murder and how it tortures them, she's powerless to lift them out of their despair, to solve the mystery for them. In the end she knows she has to let them go. Banal as it was, the bottom line was that Susie Salmon realized life was for the living and it needed to go on, despite tragedy.

And *that's* what resonated with Dane. He now thought he'd been mulling this realization, this epiphany, since he had reread the novel over Christmas break, and today, as he lectured, that theme was brought home to him as having relevance to his own life.

He glanced over at the small window in his classroom door, irrationally afraid not only that someone was peering in at him, but also that they could read his thoughts.

And what thoughts! Ever since Katy died, he'd been wondering what he should do about his secret.

Dane was gay. He always had been, from as far back as he could remember. An image flashed in his head of a very young Dane, little more than a boy really, kneeling at his bedroom window late one summer night when he couldn't sleep. The Bernards lived on a busy street that led into downtown Summitville. Back then there were often guys hitchhiking in front of Dane's house. And he would watch these young men—scruffy, usually, sometimes smoking, with their tight jeans and rebel swaggers—and would feel a curious excitement.

And then there was that one night when his father had crept up silently behind him. His deep voice had startled Dane as he knelt behind his son. "What you looking at?" And he peered over Dane's shoulder. There was nothing to see out there on the night-quiet street, really, other than what Dane now figured was a teenaged boy, dressed in ripped-up jeans and a gray tank top, waiting for a car to come by so he could beg for a ride with his thumb. He had long, shaggy hair and a wispy beard. His shoulders were broad, and his ass rode high in the faded jeans. Dane could remember him even now.

But when his father laid eyes on what Dane had been watching, he moved away silently. They never spoke of it.

But Dane had crawled back into his twin bed, face hot with deep shame, feeling caught and that there was something wrong with him. His dad had passed away not long after that—lung cancer; he smoked three packs a day—and Dane, maybe not consciously, vowed he would never feel that shame again.

So even though he might have known, on some weird subconscious level, that he was gay, he didn't *accept* it. His big size, his athletic prowess, his general manliness as he grew older, made it easy to "pass," and Dane was grateful for that ability. He felt sorry for the sissy boys he witnessed as he was growing up, those who frequented the libraries, or the glee club, or the drama society. They couldn't hide who they were. It was too constitutional for them. And although Dane never experienced the teasing and bullying those boys were subjected to, he pitied them.

But pity sometimes, in Dane's darkest hours, turned to envy. How freeing it would be, he thought, when he had no one to answer to save for himself, to just be who you were, to *not* have a choice in the matter, as he had believed he did.

But he never really did. He knew, deep down, being gay, being who he was, wasn't a choice. It hadn't ever been, even though he married his college sweetheart—and yes, he loved her with all his heart, even if it wasn't always with all his libido—even though he made a beautiful daughter and a handsome son who looked just like him. There was always that ache in the back of his mind, tugging at his heart. *I am not living the life I am meant for.* Despite all the love he got from his family, and Dane never minimized that—was never, ever ungrateful for it—he always wondered what his life would have been had he been unable to "pass."

He'd always believed he'd never be able to take off his mask. He'd made peace with it, taking comfort in the bosom of his family's love, which was no small thing.

But now, now that he no longer had a wife, now that times were different from what they were when Dane was growing up in the 1980s and '90s, maybe it wasn't too late for him to be who he really was....

A knock at the door startled him. He looked over, and it was the new guy. Dane couldn't remember his name, but he hadn't forgotten his face, sort of a nebbish, a nerd, and, Dane gulped, frighteningly cute. That face was looking in at him right now, smiling.

Dane remembered he was supposed to meet with him for a sort of orientation, to see if the new guy had any questions. Policy. Procedure. Who to trust on the faculty. Who to avoid. Stuff like that.

Dane stood, grinning, hoping he hid well enough that he'd been lost in deep reverie, and headed over to the door to open it, to welcome what's-his-name inside. Dane opened the door. "Come on in!" he said, perhaps a bit too heartily. He gambled, "Sean, is it?"

"Seth, Seth Wolcott," the new teacher corrected him.

"Sorry! I'm terrible with names, especially when I don't have a seating chart in front of me." Dane held out a hand toward the sea of plastic one-piece desk and chair units. "Make yourself at home." Dane briefly considered sitting in one of the student chairs himself, but his size prevented it from being even remotely comfortable anyway.

"It's okay," Seth said, taking a seat.

Dane collapsed into the creaking desk chair he had occupied for longer than he cared to remember and met the young man's eyes.

And something passed between them. Recognition? Attraction? It was too brief for Dane to categorize, but there was something—the gaze held just a fraction of a second longer, Dane believed, than two straight men would hold it. He felt heat rise to his face and grinned.

Seth grinned back.

And Dane wondered if he was in trouble.

CHAPTER 6

KATY HAD always done the cooking. Dane's dinner tonight was typical of the "new regime" since they'd lost her. Dane had stopped on his way home from school and picked up a rotisserie chicken, ready-to-go salad, and a box of macaroni and cheese. This was what passed for cooking. The kids seemed to like it, and he had had to admit, he did too. Anything he could throw together in a maximum of ten minutes was... delicious.

They were just finishing up, Clarissa pushing around the last morsel or two of food on her plate and Dane wondering if she was trying to make it appear she had eaten more than she actually had. He had watched her take a chicken wing, about a tablespoon of the mac and cheese, and then fill in the remainder of her plate with salad, which she ate with no dressing.

The opposite way his son ate said he either hadn't noticed his sister's borderline anorectic mealtime behavior or he was just happy to have more food for himself. He was big like his dad, and Dane remembered being Joey's age and the constant, voracious hunger that went hand in hand with growth.

Thoughts like these were helping Dane keep his mind off what he knew he really needed to be concentrating on. But his body and his gut hadn't forgotten. What little he had eaten rivaled Clarissa's consumption, but Dane knew if he ate much more, it might come back up. His stomach roiled with acid in anticipation of the news he was about to deliver.

Sure, he thought, *I can back out. I can be a chicken like the desiccated one on the table and put it off until tomorrow, next week, next month, next year. I can wait until the kids are grown and out of the house, married with children of their own. I can wait until I'm an old man.*

And then maybe I won't do it, because it won't matter anymore.

No, you need to do it now. You've waited decades. That's long enough.

Tell them. Tell them the truth.

But how?

Clarissa was first to rise from the table. Just before she got up to take her plate to the sink, scrape it off, and put it in the dishwasher, Dane heard the ping of an incoming text message. Text messages, Dane had learned, induced an almost Pavlovian response, especially in teenage girls. They could not be ignored.

"Honey, could you sit down for a minute?" Dane wondered where he found the courage to say even this much, innocuous as it was. Joey looked up from the chicken leg he was gnawing on, and Dane suspected he detected the seriousness in his father's tone. There was concern in his eyes.

"Sure, Dad," she said, rolling her eyes a bit. She'd been an absolute angel for the months after her mother's death, but some of her less-than-savory adolescent girl traits were beginning to filter back in, refusing to be denied. "But I can't talk for long. Jesse just texted me and—"

Dane cut her off with a raised palm. "Please!" He knew his voice came out a little strangled, a little desperate. He attempted a smile to soften his tone.

"I really need to talk to you guys." His stomach did a somersault. "It's important."

Clarissa sat up a little straighter, pushed her phone away. It pinged again. Dane was grateful when she shut off the sound.

"What is it, Dad? Is everything okay?"

How to say it? How does one break news like this?

Maybe an object lesson.... Not so long ago, Bruce—now Caitlyn—Jenner had been everywhere one looked. Perhaps he could use the former Olympic medalist's journey to illustrate his own parallel need to finally come to terms with who he was, to live an honest life at last.

"You guys remember Caitlyn Jenner?" He grinned, feeling cold suddenly, as though all the color were draining out of him.

Joey snickered. "That old Kardashian dude? Became a woman? He looked pretty hot on the cover of that magazine, though. I mean for an old dude."

Dane cut his gaze to his son. "Be respectful," he admonished.

Joey continued shoveling mac and cheese into his mouth.

"Anyway, I thought what he—she—did took a lot of courage. It was a very brave move."

Clarissa shoved her chair back from the table. "Dad. I really need to get back to Jesse. Is this all?"

It was Dane's turn to roll his eyes. They were going to make it difficult for him to build up to his revelation. Maybe that was good. Sort of like being pushed out of an airplane when you first skydive....

"Jenner—Caitlyn was very brave," Dane repeated and found he couldn't look at his children. He stared down at the table, feeling his breath quicken. Beads of sweat popped out on his forehead. He could feel them up there, and he swiped at them. "She had carried around something that was important to her being for so many years. I know she got lots of publicity, good and bad, and lots of money, but I still think to make the move she did, to live an honest life, was courageous. Don't you?"

"Brave? To wear women's underwear?" Joey snickered.

"Joey, please!"

"What's the point of all this?" Clarissa asked, finally glancing up from the screen on her phone.

Maybe you should do this another time. No. That would just be taking an easy out. These are kids. Another time is not going to be any different. You know that. You know them. But it's time to take off the gloves. Maybe the object lesson would be good in a classroom, but a family kitchen? Forget it! Dane chuckled to himself. That seemed to get their attention. Both of them looked up.

"What?" Clarissa asked.

Dane blew out a big sigh. *Out with it.* "I was talking about Jenner to make a point. Jenner the man waited until he was sixty-five to come out—"

"Wait a minute! Dad's gonna tell us he's gonna become a woman!" Joey said, and both he and his sister collapsed in laughter.

This was not going the way Dane anticipated. At all.

"Yeah. He'll need, like, size seventeen pumps!"

That tickled the two of them even more. Dane just stared.

When his children saw he was not joining them in the hilarity, their laughter dried up quickly. Clarissa's mouth dropped open.

"You're not. Are you? I mean, transitioning...."

Dane shook his head. "What do you think? I'd make a hideous woman. What I'm trying to say, Joey, Clarissa, is that I've had feelings for many years. *Not* feelings that I was in the wrong body, but feelings that I hid away, mostly from myself, but also from everyone I knew, including your mom."

He regarded his children at the table. Any vestige of joking or laughter had left their faces. He was certain they had no idea what was coming, but he wondered if there was something, instinctive maybe, within them that told them to brace themselves.

In the end there was no way to say it other than just to say it. He felt a curious sensation—a tightening inside. He felt he was steeling himself. He breathed out—*whoosh*—and said it. "I'm gay."

Joey picked up a radish from his salad and flung it at him. "You are *not*! Dude, please!"

Clarissa shoved back her chair. "This has all been very fun, although I'm not certain I understand the point of it, but can I go to my room now? *Please.*"

Dane reached out, took Joey's hand, took Clarissa's. "Kids. I'm serious. This is something I've struggled against my whole life. Losing your mom has made me see how little time we have, and I just can't live a lie anymore."

Clarissa snatched her hand away. She looked up at him with wounded eyes. "Just to be sure. You're not punking us here? This isn't a joke?"

Dane shook his head.

There was something snide to her tone, but underneath that Dane could read hope. Hope that he'd confirm he was having them on, kidding around.

"It's not a joke. This doesn't change anything. I'm still your dad, still the same guy. I'm still here for you. I still love you—with every fiber of my being."

Clarissa stood up from the table so fast her chair toppled over to the tile floor behind her. Dane could see she was shaking, and it made his heart ache.

"It doesn't change anything?" Her voice went up high. "It doesn't change anything? Are you out of your mind? It changes everything!"

She screeched this last bit, but Dane could see unshed tears standing in her eyes.

God. I should have kept this to myself. What's said can never be unsaid. What have I done? What Pandora's box have I opened? Dane said softly, "You're right. It changes things. Changes who you thought I was, and that's not small. But what I was trying to say—badly, I guess—was that it doesn't change what's essential—my love for you and your brother. The fact that I will be here for you both, always."

Clarissa was shaking her head. "You're unbelievable. Fucking unbelievable."

Even Joey's mouth dropped open as he stared, slack-jawed, at his sister. "Chill. Can't you see this is hard for him?"

Dane looked over at his son. He was still holding his hand, and Joey smiled at him and squeezed. The tiny gesture made Dane want to cry. If you had asked him, before he told them this essential truth, which kid would have a problem with it, Joey was the one he would have picked.

"Hard for *him?*" Clarissa's lips nearly vanished into a thin horizontal line.

Dane always thought the descriptor of someone's eyes blazing was hyperbole, purple prose, but now in his daughter's brown eyes, he saw it really happen.

"Please, honey," Dane said, reaching out with his other hand.

43

She backed away, looking down at his hand with horror, as if it was diseased. "No! No! So, what? You used Mom all these years to hide behind?"

She took a couple more steps back toward the kitchen's exit. "And what? Now that she's gone, you can be free to be your faggot self?"

"Stop it!" Joey cried. "That's too harsh."

Dane didn't know what to say and cursed himself for it. Mutely, he looked from one child to the other.

Clarissa turned and walked out of the room, calling over her shoulder, "The only thing that's harsh is finding out we have a liar for a dad."

Dane slumped. Joey pulled his hand away, but only to pat his dad's shoulder.

"She doesn't mean it. She's just, um, like, surprised, you know?" He squeezed Dane's shoulder. "It is an awful lot to take in. Dude, are you sure?"

Dane made himself look at his son. He nodded. "I'm sure."

They sat in silence like that for a moment, until the slam of Clarissa's bedroom door upstairs caused them both to jump. Dane looked to his son and grinned at him, feeling helpless and sheepish. "I guess I could have handled that better, huh? Are you okay?"

Joey got up from the table and began clearing their dinner stuff away, hauling it over to the sink to be put in the dishwasher. "I'm okay, Dad. It's your life."

"I know. I know, but it's a lot for you to accept. I just want you to know that I'll always—first and foremost—be your father."

Joey finished up loading the dishwasher and rinsed his hands off. He sat back down at the table. "Look. I don't know if I get what being gay is all about, I mean, when girls are so hot and all. Why would you look twice at a guy?"

Joey shivered, but he was smiling. His expression turned serious again, and it tore at Dane's heart to realize his little boy was trying to comfort him.

"It's no big deal, man. I'd be lying if I said I wanted to think about it. But who wants to think about their parents and sex together anyway? Yuck! But I'm glad you're honest with us, glad you trust us enough to tell us."

"Thank you," Dane said with a shuddering breath, barely above a whisper. He was trying his best not to cry. "I don't know what's going to happen," Dane confessed. And he didn't. "I just didn't want you guys to have some image of me that wasn't true. What kind of example would I be if I let that continue?"

"I don't know, Dad. I'm twelve." He leaned over and hugged his father, patting his back.

Dane laughed, laughed until the tears came. "Oh, Joey," he said, when he could get his breath. "What would I do without you?"

The boy shrugged. "I don't know. Mow the lawn yourself?" He started out of the kitchen. "I got homework. Science."

"That's it, then? No questions?"

Joey stopped and looked at him, eyebrows coming together in confusion. He cocked his head. "Not really. Not right now." He left the room.

And came back in a second later. "I love you, Dad."

And was gone again.

Dane called out after him, "I love you too, son."

He looked at the empty table before him. His big moment was weirdly anticlimactic. But he felt that was a deception. They had crossed a line. Nothing would ever be the same again.

Part of him felt free. The other part was terrified.

And all he could think of was how tired he suddenly was.

DANE AWOKE with a gasp, heart pounding, as if a loud noise had startled him. His sheets were damp with sweat, even though he could see snowflakes coming gently down outside his bedroom window.

The house was quiet. The only noise was that of their gas heating system clicking on and off. Dane glanced over at the charging dock/alarm clock on his nightstand and saw it was a little after 5:00 a.m.

The dream came back to him all at once.

He's in a room he doesn't recognize. It's silent and stark—white walls, hardwood floors shining dully in the gleam of recessed lighting. The room has no windows, no pictures on the walls, no decoration whatsoever.

In the middle of the room is a plain chair, a ladder-back type that would go with a dining set. And on it, facing away from him, sits a woman.

Dane lets out a cry, yet no sound actually emerges from his mouth. The silence of the room is more like a roaring of blood in his ears, so loud it drowns everything else out. But his cry is genuine because he recognizes the back of that head, the shape of those shoulders, the simple white quilted robe she wears.

It's his wife, Katy.

He calls to her, but again can make no sound. She doesn't turn. His heart leaps, and he quickens his pace toward the chair in which she sits, so still, so still. He's longed to see her face one last time. Will he get his chance now?

He rounds the figure on the chair. But when he gets to the other side, all he can see—once more—is the back of her.

That was when he awoke. That was when he felt startled, when the dream, he now realized, morphed into nightmare.

What did it mean?

Dane sat up in bed, staring at the snow coming down in lazy whorls outside his window. The sky was lightening, a shade of slate, blue-gray, just a little bit lighter than full-on night. He waited as his breathing, heart rate, and respiration returned to normal. He thought of his wife. She had never appeared to him, as far as Dane could remember, since her accident at the end of last summer. There had been times when he wished she would have, when he could have told her things, asked for her counsel in raising the kids—especially last night at dinner. And he did talk to her, here and there, when no one else was around. But sadly there was never any sense of her, any feeling that she watched over him and the kids, that she listened.

Yet she came to him in a dream. But why could he only see the back of her head? If she was going to appear to him, why appear in such an inaccessible way?

46

Or had she really appeared to him at all? Was this simply his subconscious crying out? Perhaps, in the back of his mind, when he confessed to the kids earlier about his sexual orientation, he was also confessing to Katy, who, he would guess, had never suspected a thing. There may have been some distance between them now and then, toward the end. And the sex certainly got a lot less frequent, but from what Dane heard, that was common among all couples, no matter on which side their bread was buttered.

But maybe, in some way, he had wanted her to know the truth about him, *of* him. To know, once and for all, the real him. Because he did truly love Katy. And how could she love him, fully and completely, if she had never really known who he was?

He remembered one time, the two of them up late in the family room and watching an episode of *The Golden Girls* together before they headed off to bed. It had been a kind of ritual with them. Dane recalled being a little more tense than usual as they laughed through another adventure in the lives of the Miami ladies of a certain age. It was because the episode had concerned a friend of Dorothy's, a lesbian, and the impact her secret had on all the girls. Dorothy had asked her mother, Sophia, how she would react if one of her kids were gay. Of course the wisecracking Sophia immediately told her daughter to "stick with what you know." But then Dorothy pressed her for a real answer. And Sophia told Dorothy something along the lines of how she wouldn't love her child one bit less, that she would wish them all the happiness in the world.

"How would you feel if Joey or Clarissa turns out to be gay?" Dane asked Katy, wondering if the question was really more about him than it was about his kids.

Katy looked at him for a long time, a glimmer of a smile playing about her lips. She closed the cover on her iPad. "I think I'd feel the same as old Sophia," she said. "It wouldn't change anything. When you really love someone, something like that doesn't matter, does it? You'd still, as Sophia says, wish them all the happiness in the world." She smiled. "Family is family."

Dane joked about Katy's answer—"And you're not even Italian!"—and then said, "You're a good mom." He looked back at the screen. Blanche had come into the bedroom, confusing the term lesbian with Lebanese and proclaiming that Danny Thomas was one. He and Katy laughed, but Dane couldn't get it out of his head that this would be the perfect quiet moment to tell this woman he had loved for so long the essential truth about himself. But all he did was meet Katy's eyes for a moment and say, "And a good wife."

"I'm very understanding," Katy said and then laughed. "If I do say so myself."

Now Dane lay back against his pillows, feeling the bed was vast and empty, and even though he was a big man, he was much too small to fill it. He wondered if Katy had the same thing on her mind that night as he did. Maybe that's why she said something—"I'm very understanding"—that was so out of character for her, a little too self-congratulatory. Perhaps she wasn't looking to highlight her own good nature, but to open a door.

Dane had missed the opportunity. And now he'd never have the chance for her to know him for who he really was.

He rose from the bed, wincing a little when his bare feet hit the hardwood floor. It was cold. "And maybe it's better she never did," he said aloud to the room, which was lightening, the furniture taking on more shape and definition as the sun rose higher. "Most wives, no matter how understanding, would not be thrilled with the news that dear hubby is a 'mo."

He got up and moved to the back of his bedroom door, where his old plaid flannel robe hung off a hook. He shrugged into it and then went back to the bed to slide into the shearling-lined Ugg slippers Katy had bought him last Christmas. They felt like heaven on his cold feet.

It was time to get the kids up.

He knocked on each of their bedroom doors, saying the same thing he did every day, "Rise and shine! Rise and shine!"

Then he moved to the top of the staircase to wait. He had learned never to assume they would get up. In a couple of minutes, Joey's door opened and his boy emerged in Spider-Man pajamas he was probably too old for but which Dane figured he was still not ready to give up. His blond hair spiked in several different directions, and his face was cross. He rubbed an eye with one hand. Dane thought the only thing that would make this picture complete was if Joey dragged a teddy bear behind him with the other hand. He smiled. Dane knew Joey was simply trying to get used to being awake once again. Dane laughed. "Go ahead down and start up the coffeepot for me, okay, sport?"

Joey nodded and tromped down the stairs. Dane called after him, "I'm thinking Eggos this morning. Okay?"

Clarissa had still not emerged. Dane knocked on her door once again. "Honey? Time to get up. We gotta be out of here in less than an hour. I'll drive you to school today, okay?" Dane was attempting to be as normal as possible, hoping if he moved ahead almost as though their dinnertime revelations hadn't happened, maybe Clarissa would too.

He tapped again on her door. "Clarissa?"

It wasn't like her not to come out. Dane felt a little frisson of nerves. Had he damaged his relationship with her irreparably?

He placed his hand on the knob and opened the door a crack… and then a little more.

The room was empty, the bed made up as though it had never been slept in.

Dane shook his head. He saw Clarissa had left him a note. It was propped up against one of the pillow shams.

Went to Jerri Lynn's for the night. Couldn't stay here.

That was all it said. Cold. Utilitarian. It tugged at Dane's heart, making him feel sad and ashamed.

He held the note in his hand, next to his daughter's bed, staring down at it for a long time until Joey called up the stairs, "Dad? Coffee's ready! You want blueberry or plain waffles?"

Dane set the note back in its place and headed for the stairs.

CHAPTER 7

THE BULLETIN board was the first thing anyone saw when he or she entered through the massive front doors of Summitville High School. It was hard to miss, positioned opposite the entry. It was large, maybe four feet by six feet, and was usually decorated to match the season, an upcoming holiday, or a big game. But today, Truman noticed as he trudged into the building after first bell, stomping his snow-covered feet on the big black rubber mat inside the front door, the bulletin board was all about *him*.

He paused for just a moment, skin prickling from more than mere cold. *Oh no, not again....* He had the odd sensation where he couldn't believe his eyes, thinking the workings of his brain were playing tricks on him. He also desperately did not want to believe what was in front of him, plain as the nose on his face.

He laughed. That was his first reaction. But it was an uncomfortable, sickly kind of laugh. He looked over his shoulder. Other kids were pouring in, allowing the icy air to sweep into the school's vestibule. None seemed to notice what had Truman so transfixed.

At least not yet.

But soon they would. And there would be laughter and pointing. And Truman, amidst it all, the center of things, the butt of the joke, would stand frozen, unable to move. It would be akin to the opening scene of the movie *Carrie* all over again, but with Truman in the shower.

He thought briefly of turning and running. His mom, who had dropped him off only moments before, might still be within the sound of his voice, especially with having to drive cautiously in consideration of the snow and ice on the roads. Could he run fast enough to catch their beater?

But what would she do? Comfort him once more with words? Tell him he was special? That he was loved? They were nice sentiments, and he loved his mom for saying them so consistently and reliably.

50

But they couldn't erase the horror of what was before him. Couldn't wipe out the cruelty trying to masquerade as comedy.

Truman looked around, and still no one noticed the images pinned to the bulletin board. But it was only a matter of time.

He ducked his head and hunched his shoulders and escaped back out the front doors like a wraith, like something invisible.

Whether or not he could catch his mom, the advantage in leaving now was being anywhere else but *here*. Even with bitter cold and frigid winds raging outside, it was warmer outside than in *here*.

DANE HAD spent a good fifteen minutes in the parking lot, bouncing up and down to ward off the icy winds blowing all around him, to see if Clarissa showed up. He needed to talk to her before beginning his day. He didn't mean to chew her out for slipping out of the house the night before. Jerri Lynn Masterson was Clarissa's best friend and had been since fifth grade. The Mastersons lived only a few houses down from them, on the same street. Dane wasn't upset that Clarissa had gone to sleep over at their house, which wasn't uncommon. But he knew her absence from the house this morning had to be related to their conversation last night.

He didn't like that she had sneaked out, even if she did leave a note, presumably so he wouldn't worry.

But either Clarissa had gotten to school before him, which was okay, or she was skipping today, which was not. Once the final bell rang, Dane knew he needed to get inside to deal with his homeroom, take attendance, listen to the morning announcements, say the Pledge of Allegiance along with the rest of the class.

Just like any other day.

Except it wasn't.

He trudged inside and saw the bulletin board. Gasped. Stopped in his tracks. There were a few kids gathered around it, nudging each other and giggling. One of them, a red-haired boy named Kimmel, whispered to his friends. All Dane heard was the dreaded "Mr. Bernard." It was enough to make the kids scatter.

It was after the final bell, and now the school's vestibule was empty. Dane neared the bulletin board, wanting a better look at what it was that cracked the students up first thing in the morning. "Oh no," he whispered as he stepped closer to the bulletin board, the images pinned to it becoming clearer.

Someone had done a tribute of sorts to Truman Reid. They must have found every yearbook photo and every school newspaper picture and done some Photoshop work on them. Here was Truman's head on the body of a sequin-gowned woman. There was Truman's face over Miley Cyrus's, swinging on an iconic wrecking ball, scantily clad. Check out the cover of *Vogue* upon which Caitlyn Jenner had come out to the world, except now Truman's replaced Jenner's face. There were scores of other photos, each of them showing poor Truman Reid in the most feminine light possible. The Photoshop work was impeccable and had obviously taken some skill and time.

So had the cruelty.

Across the top of the montage of photos was a large white banner with screaming red letters. It read:

"Tru-woman Reid! We love you dearly, sweet thang!"

Dane felt his heart clench in outrage for the kid, hoping against hope the boy hadn't seen the display. Dane began ripping the images from the board's cork surface, looking around him almost guiltily, as if he himself were the culprit. He shredded the images, wishing he got more satisfaction as he watched them drift to the snow-wet and muddy tile floor.

Finally, when the bulletin board was bare, Dane stood, wondering what was wrong with these kids, why they got such pleasure in being mean. Where were their hearts? Where was their empathy? Their compassion? Dane didn't want to believe these were qualities that took until the age of, say, eighteen to develop. He shook his head, wondering what effect this would have on Truman if he had indeed been unfortunate enough to see the display.

He didn't have long to wonder.

Betsy Wagner rushed up to him, the hurt and terror in her green eyes magnified by the lenses in her glasses. She was a little out of breath. "Dane. Dane, oh God, I'm glad you're here."

"What's the matter, Bets?"

"We have a situation." She grabbed his hand and started moving away. "Outside. On the roof."

TRUMAN SHIVERED, teeth chattering, clutching his arms about his thin body. The view from the rooftop was stunning, never mind that pain and despair had brought him up there. He stood on the west tower of the school, and its flat bottom allowed for better footing, although when Truman considered why he'd come up there in the first place, that really wasn't much of a consideration.

But being able to stand still, to look out and think without the fear of sliding off an icy slope, was worth something. Truman wanted his last few moments on earth to be serene instead of filled with pain and humiliation. He wanted to be in control for once in his life.

Which is why he appreciated the secure footing. And the view, once his tears cleared away and allowed him to focus, was something to appreciate. Truman felt as though he was seeing the landscape for the first time, as if the tears had cleansed his vision.

Summitville High School was built at the top of a hill, so the lookout over the surrounding valley and Ohio River was stunning. But from up here, that "stunning" aspect was multiplied one hundredfold—or something like that; math had never been Truman's strong suit. From this vantage point, he could witness the slow brownish green curve of the river, the tree-dotted hills of Ohio on one side and the northern panhandle of West Virginia on the other. He imagined himself and Odd Thomas making their way along the banks of that river in happier times. He pictured himself beside the river, meeting up with someone special in the lavender light of dusk. But he didn't want to think about that now…. He didn't want to think about *that* ever again.

Mimicking the river's flow were the roadways and streets that networked through the Ohio valley with cars and trucks hurrying in every direction, showing Truman that so many people had so many places to go. Yet all he could imagine was going *down*. He leaned over to the rail at the edge of the roof and peered down into the faculty parking lot at the concrete and the snow-covered economy cars and trucks filling every available space. Jutting out just below was another ledge, sticking out only a little less than the one he leaned against. Truman would have to make sure he missed that on the way down.

What would it feel like? Would he finally understand what it felt like to fly, if only for a second or two?

Would it hurt when he landed? Or would shock or some other built-in kindness block the pain?

He sucked in a breath that seemed to crystallize in his lungs—it was that icy.

All around the valley were homes of various shapes and sizes, businesses too, most all of them small until you got to the outskirts of town, off the highway, where fast-food joints clustered around the town's Mecca—Walmart. He smiled bitterly when he thought of how he and his mom thought they were living high on the hog when they felt they could afford to shop there, to buy *brand spankin' new*, as Patsy would say.

Pathetic.

Never mind. The people filling all these stores, restaurants, cars, houses, all of them—if they knew Truman or knew of him—hated him or, at the very least, didn't give two shits about him. He was someone of whom no one was afraid to ask, with a grin dancing about his or her lips, if he was a boy or a girl. And when he would respond with "boy," they thought it was just a scream to wonder, "Are you sure?"

What was the point of living if you were simply the butt of all jokes? What was the point when your purpose in life seemed to be to provide an object of ridicule and amusement for the rest of the world? What was the point when no one, save for one's mother—and how sad was that?—seemed to care if you lived or died? What was the point when you were *not* being teased or called names like pansy, pussy, sissy, fag, piss willy, queer, or *her*, you were being used as a punching bag for the sport and amusement of the more athletically inclined of your classmates?

What was the frigging point?

And what was the point of finding—at last—someone you loved, only to have that love thrown back in your face like a discarded rubber? But again, Truman didn't want to go *there*. He wouldn't allow himself to think about *him*.

Truman didn't know the point of anything. He knew only there was no purpose in going on, in living. Why live if it only brought you pain? As he stared out at the windswept and snow-buried landscape beneath him, his sole regret was the knowledge of how sad this would make Patsy. His breath caught, and fresh tears rose to his eyes as he imagined her leaning over his battered and crushed body on the concrete, hysterical and having to be pulled away. He could see her face, the pain in her eyes, her anguish, and it did make him pause. *Can I really do that to her when I know how much she loves me? It will kill her too.*

Truman shook his head. She would move on. The sad truth was, Truman's being gone would not kill Patsy. Sure, she'd be in pain for a while, but then, but then.... She'd be better off. She would be freer without him, without the burden of having such a misfit underfoot.

Right?

He catalogued all the slights he had endured since the beginning of the school year back in August. There was the posting of gay news items and, worse, gay porn to his Facebook page, so many posts that Truman had finally shut down the page, no longer able to be a part of the social network that seemed to bind so many of the kids together. There was the time when a contingent of boys had caught him after school, perhaps inspired by an old repeat of one of Truman's favorite television shows, *Glee*, and stuffed him into a dumpster behind the school. Truman had lain in the stinking garbage—it had been late September and still warm outside—until he heard their laughter die down as they walked away. Truman was pretty sure things would be even worse for him if he managed to climb out while they were still there.

And then there was the time he came late to gym class just as his teacher, the ironically named Mr. Nicely, was talking about him, a grin lifting his mustache playfully, unaware that Truman stood just inside the doorway not three feet away. What was the name Mr. Nicely had so kindly endowed Truman with? Oh yeah, *Twinkletoes.*

Hilarious.

Truman had even stopped going to the cafeteria at lunchtime because there wasn't a single table where he was welcome. He tried sitting alone for a while but tired of the stares and the occasional carrot stick flung his way. He ended up spending his lunch period in a carrel at the library, reading. At least he'd managed to work his way through all the Harry Potter books, plus the complete literary output of Neil Gaiman. For all the literary nourishment, he'd been starving by the time he got home.

He swung himself up on the ledge that ran around the edge of the roof and sat down on it, legs dangling. A dangerous sense of vertigo rose up, and it caused a flutter in his chest. Again he told himself that the silver lining to this very dark cloud was that the drop would be his chance to see what it felt like to fly. Defy gravity. And when he landed? He imagined it could only hurt for a second or two. When he crashed into the concrete three stories below, crushing bones and organs, he would be pretty much obliterated. Oblivious. And wasn't the idea of oblivion a lovely one? It would be over, blessedly—all the pain, the suffering, the loneliness, the name-calling, that feeling of being different.

He would be out of it.

And Truman could think of no finer place to be.

He scooted forward on the ledge.

"HE'S UP there!" Betsy pointed to Truman on the roof ledge, her voice high with hysteria. "You have to do something, Dane!"

Dane peered up, squinting. For a moment he could see nothing. Although the day was bitter cold, with the temperature in the single digits and, with the wind chill factored in, most likely below zero, the sun was blinding and bright. The sky was a brilliant cerulean blue. The anxiousness and terror in Betsy's voice ramped up his own terror, making him feel like an animal being plunged into nightmare.

Quickly, his eyes adjusted to the sun's glare, and he could make out a silhouette on top of one of the two towers that fronted the school, one on either side, like a castle. A small figure with its legs dangling casually over the ledge flung Dane's heart into his throat. Out of the corner of his mouth, he whispered desperately to Betsy, "Who is it?"

"It's Truman Reid."

"Oh God. Of course it is." Dane flashed back to only a short time ago and what he had witnessed on the school's central bulletin board. *He must have seen.* The kid was desperate. Dane recollected that it seemed like almost every week, maybe even every day, the boy was the punching bag for a bully, the butt of a joke, or a target for derision. Dane tried to step in when he could, but he couldn't be everywhere at once. With staff cutbacks and growing class sizes, it had become harder and harder for Dane to concentrate on individual students, no matter how compassionate he wanted to be or how much they needed him.

And today, right now, Truman Reid needed someone.

He let out a shuddering breath and reached for Betsy's hand, clutching it for a moment and squeezing for courage. "What do I say to him? What do I *say*?" Dane felt on the verge of tears. There was a quivering in his gut that made him feel dizzy, as though it were he and not the boy dangling over the edge of that rooftop. His next few words could, quite literally, mean the difference between life and death.

Betsy Wagner, teacher of social studies and human sexuality, could be relied upon for her well of knowledge in a desperate situation. She leaned in and whispered, "Hell if I know."

Dane turned away from Truman for a moment to glare at her.

"But you'll think of something. All the kids trust you," she said, and Dane was sure the smile she gave him was meant to be reassuring, if not inspiring.

Like Truman, Dane once again found himself alone. Betsy stepped back and away from him, presumably to give him more space to conjure up just the right words, the magic speech that would coerce the kid into swinging his legs back *slowly* off the ledge and then to retrace his steps back inside the school, where he could get the help he needed.

Dane put a hand up to shield his eyes from the sun. "Truman?" he yelled. "Truman? Can I just talk to you, man?"

A shadow fell across the ground to Dane's left as someone stepped up next to him. He turned quickly and saw it was Seth Wolcott, the new teacher. Seth's hazel eyes, behind his glasses, seemed darker with concern. He handed Dane a bullhorn. "We had this in the theater department. Thought you could use it." Seth clamped a hand on Dane's shoulder and squeezed. The simple touch gave Dane courage.

Dane lifted the bullhorn to his mouth, grateful for the amplification. He only hoped he could hear if and when Truman responded.

"Truman?" he repeated. "I just want to talk to you. Okay?" He glanced behind him, stunned to see a massive crowd had formed. It appeared the whole school stood outside now, behind him. It was both a comfort, a horror, and eerie, because there was no sound from any of them. Dane hadn't even heard them assemble.

He whispered to Seth, "Has anyone called 911?" Dane longed for official help. He also feared it—the sound of a siren could startle poor Truman right off the roof.

Seth answered, "Betsy called a few minutes ago from her cell. Someone should be here soon."

For now, though, silence prevailed. Dane lifted the bullhorn to his lips once more. "Listen, son, whatever's got you up there is something bad. I'm not gonna kid around with you or insult your intelligence by pretending otherwise. Life has dealt you a raw hand, and that really sucks."

Oh God. This is terrible. I can't make this speech. I can't. Where are all the wise words from the books I teach?

Dane drew in a quivering breath and called up, "But whatever it is, the one thing I know, and I think you know too, deep in your heart, is that nothing stays the same. *Nothing*, Truman. There's no one on God's green earth who can say what's gonna happen tomorrow. Or even a few minutes from now. We just don't know." Dane looked up at the boy's silhouette, unmoving, above. Was he getting through at all?

"Truman? Can you just throw me a bone and let me know that you hear me, son?"

Dane waited, figuring he'd give the boy some space in which to reply. The wait seemed to go on for hours, when Dane's rational mind told him it was only seconds until he heard the boy's high and thin voice filter down.

"I hear you."

Dane shut his eyes for a moment, feeling immense gratitude for such a small gift. "I'm glad you can *hear*. But can you *listen*?"

"I'm not going anywhere... yet," Truman called down.

Dane was relieved to see the tiny trace of humor in his response. Gallows humor, but it was better than nothing.

"Then listen to me. What you're thinking of is an end. There'll be no coming back. What you're doing is taking hope out of the equation. What you'd be doing, if you jump or even accidentally slide off that roof, is removing any chance at all for things getting better."

"They always say 'It gets better,' but they lie," Truman screamed. "Nothing ever changes!"

"Truman, you're too young to be so pessimistic. *Everything* changes. Constantly. Whether we want it to or not. Things go from bad to worse, from good to better, and everywhere in between. And most of the time, none of it makes sense." Dane paused and reminded himself to *breathe*. "Do you remember last fall?" Dane wished he'd said autumn to describe the season.

"What about it?" Truman asked, inching closer to the edge.

Dane wanted to gasp, wanted to scream, wanted to hand the bullhorn to Seth or Betsy, but he gripped it with knuckles gone bloodless. In the distance he heard the wail of a siren. How stupid! He wished the cops or the ambulance or whatever it was would arrive silently, which would make sense, which would be respectful.

"It's when I, uh, lost my wife. Mrs. Bernard? You remember? She was in a car accident?"

"I'm so sorry," Truman called down.

"Thank you. But my point is that when I got up that morning, I didn't know my life was going to take a turn that was, well, *cataclysmic*." Dane paused. "Yeah, it was really bad. But that's not my point. My point is, life can turn on a dime. Something could happen tomorrow that could change everything, believe me. And you wouldn't be here to see it. Don't rob yourself of that chance. Don't take away possibility."

Truman didn't say anything. Dane looked around him once more, hoping to see Seth Wolcott, but as far as he could tell, the new teacher was no longer in the crowd. Dane felt disappointed. He wanted Seth there for moral support, if nothing more.

Dane swallowed hard. The words about hope, about possibility, didn't seem to be getting through. *At least he hasn't jumped. Not yet, anyway.* Dane felt as though the clock was ticking down, faster with each passing second. He thought his life had winnowed down to this one essential moment, when he had the power to change everything in someone's life—or not.

He blew out a breath. Common ground. That's what he needed. That could make all the difference. "Truman? I know what you're going through."

"Yeah, right," Truman shot back, bitter.

"No. No, I do. I know what it's like to be different." *Oh fuck, just say it.* Dane tried to draw in some courage along with the freezing air. "I know what it's like to be gay."

"Oh, what would you know about it?" Truman asked. A bitter laugh floated earthward on a cold downdraft.

"Everything, Truman. I know everything, because I'm just like you in that department."

The silence in the crowd broke behind Dane. There was a murmur and questioning voices. He wondered if Clarissa was in the crowd. He wondered how many people would believe him and how many would think he was just using the admission as a ruse to con a desperate kid off the roof. He didn't care really who thought what, as long as Truman believed him.

"Right. You're gay?"

At least Dane had gotten Truman to laugh. He took a couple of steps forward, craning his neck and squinting to see the boy, backlit by the sun above him. "I am. I just came to terms with it myself, Truman. You're, like, the third person I've told." Dane laughed, feeling even more on the edge of hysteria. "Well, when you consider the crowd down here, I guess you're more like the *four hundred* and third person I've told.

"But it's true. I'm gay, just like you. And believe me, I know how hard that can be to accept. Hell, it's taken me all my life.

"And Truman?" Dane felt tears well up in his eyes then, and his subsequent words broke a little as he shouted them upward, through a fucking bullhorn. "Truman, I can't speak for you. But I can speak for myself. This is hard for me, confusing. I need someone to talk to, someone who understands.

"Truman! Truman!" Dane found it hard to speak. But he needed to go on, as much for himself as Truman. "Can you be that person for me?" Dane choked back the tears.

Truman was silent; the crowd had reverted back to silence too. An icy wind blew out of the north, and it made Dane's teeth chatter.

Finally, a word from Truman. "You're fuckin' with me, right?"

Dane laughed. "No. No way, man. You think I'd say something like that, lay myself open like this in front of all these people I have to work with, have to teach, have to see every single day, if it weren't true?"

There was a pause as Truman presumably considered what Dane said. "I guess not."

"Will you come down, Truman? Can I talk to you? If you don't need my help, it's okay. But I need yours. I really do." And Dane realized the simple truth of what he said.

A cloud had moved across the sun, throwing shadows across Dane and the spectators. The temperature plunged a few more degrees. But having the sun out of the way also made it easier to see Truman, his body more defined.

Dane watched him as he wiggled back on the ledge, swinging his legs back, trying to position himself—Dane hoped and prayed—to get off that ledge.

And it looked like he was going to make it. Every backward motion Truman made indicated Dane's words had had some effect and that he was going to get down from up there.

Truman had almost made it to the point where he could turn and safely swing his legs over the edge when he slipped.

And in an instant he was airborne, no longer on the roof.

Dane was too startled to scream. He jammed a fist into his mouth.

A siren gave a piercing *whoop* just behind him as the paramedics arrived.

CHAPTER 8

DANE'S HORROR turned to qualified relief as a figure rushed out from behind the boy and hooked his arms underneath Truman's armpits, preventing him from the long, surely fatal fall to the concrete below.

Dane's heart hammered in his chest so hard he feared it was the onset of an attack.

Like everyone else in the crowd, he peered upward at the drama unfolding. The sun was still obscured by a heavy bank of gray clouds, so Dane could see who had snuck up behind Truman. It was Seth.

Thank God for Seth.

But Truman wasn't safe yet. His whole body still dangled precariously from the rooftop. He wasn't helping matters by kicking his legs, surely a panicked reaction. The hold Seth had on the boy was tenuous, and Dane knew the simple law of gravity was not working in Seth's favor. The strain on his back, his arms, and his psyche must be incredible at the moment. It would be all too easy, Dane knew, for Truman to slip from Seth's fingers. Or worse, for gravity to pull them both over the edge....

Dane couldn't see well enough to make out much detail in their faces, but Dane imagined Seth as red and breathless, the strain of trying to keep this slight boy from falling an incredible challenge. He also imagined the terror that must be lighting up Truman's features. Dane wanted to believe the boy had changed his mind and was coming back when he slipped—accidentally.

"Pull him back!" someone cried.

"You can do it, Mr. Wolcott!" someone else yelled.

"Let the faggot fall!" another voice added. Dane's head whipped around and glared at the crowd of mostly students behind him. Although there'd been a few titters at the remark, it wasn't apparent who'd uttered it.

"Truman, we love you!" someone else shouted, and Dane felt his faith in humanity restored just a little bit.

Dane lifted the bullhorn. "You can do it, guys. Just don't panic." *Easy for you to say!* "Slow and steady. Slow and steady."

And Dane's breathing, respiration, and heart rate slowed, timed with the rescue. Seth managed, at last, to pull Truman back from the edge. He got him to his feet. Once he had the boy secure, Seth's arms wrapped protectively around his chest, the crowd burst into cheers, applause, and whistles.

And Dane smiled, even though his knees were so weak he feared he would simply drop to the ground. He felt a rush of giddy relief course though him that made him want to alternately laugh and sob. His hands were trembling, and he flexed them to try to quell the tremors.

Seth leaned forward with one arm still around the boy. He raised his other arm and gave the crowd a thumbs-up, which incited a whole new wave of cheers and whistles.

Dane watched as Truman and Seth moved back and away from the ledge, heading, Dane was certain, for the door at the back. And the stairs… oh God yes, the stairs.

Dane turned away once Seth and Truman were out of view. He didn't know what would happen next. He wasn't surprised to see the crowd beginning to disperse as people headed back inside the building. Principal Calhoun urged everyone to get back inside and to "Keep it orderly."

The cold helped push everyone back inside the school's warm embrace.

But then Dane noticed two things that surprised him, although they shouldn't have.

The first was that official help had arrived, presumably heralded by sirens. Dane had been so caught up in the drama and the peril, he couldn't recall noticing the red-and-white ambulance and the black police car. Right now EMTs were folding up a large net to put back in the ambulance and talking to one another. Their words were snatched up by the wind and carried away before Dane could hear them. The sight of the net—and the possibility of what could have happened—

made Dane shiver and caused a splash of acid to jet up from his stomach to his throat.

The second thing Dane noticed, and this was almost simultaneous with the first, was a young woman rushing toward him. At first he thought she was a student. Her slight figure and dark curly hair belied her age until she was practically standing right before him. She wore tight jeans and a cropped ski jacket. Big gold hoops dangled from her ears. Too much makeup.

But in spite of the party-girl appearance, her face was a mask of desperation. It was this last that made Dane realize who she probably was.

"Are you Mr. Bernard?"

"Yes." Dane tried to smile, but at the moment he found he was incapable.

"The school called me, said you were trying to talk my baby down from the roof." She swallowed hard, and Dane could see she was trying not to collapse into sobs. She looked wildly about her—at the parking lot, at the EMTs and cops finishing up, calm after the storm.

Her gaze finally returned to him. "I'm Patsy. Patsy Reid, Truman's mom."

"Oh, of course!" Still, she seemed almost too young to be Truman's mother. "I think we met before. Last fall? PTA?"

Patsy waved his questions away impatiently. "Is he okay?" she wanted to know, a little breathless. "Where is he?" And then she did break into a short burst of tears, her mouth open in an anguished O. Finally she asked, her voice a plaintive plea, "Why would he do this? Why?"

Acting on instinct, Dane quickly gathered her up in his arms and stroked her hair. "He's had a lot to deal with. I suspect it all just became too much. But he saw sense. He should be out any minute."

She pushed back, away, probably not ready for comfort. "They said you saved him. They said you turned things around." Her eyes grew big with fear. "They said he was ready to jump."

She actually hit herself in the chest, hard, one, two, three times. "It hurts me here to think he would do that. I haven't been able to give

64

him much, but I always gave him all I had. I always tried to be the best mom I could!"

"I know, I know." Dane reached out and patted her shoulder. He looked behind him.

Seth and Truman emerged from the building. Seth had his arm around Truman. Both of their faces were white, and Dane wasn't sure which of the two looked more shell-shocked.

Patsy let out a hoarse combination of a sob and a wail and dashed toward her son, arms outstretched. She snatched him up and held him close, stroking his hair for all she was worth.

Seth stood away. Dane didn't move.

Both were silent until one of the EMTs came up to mother and son. Dane couldn't hear every word the young woman said, but he caught enough to understand that they wanted to take Truman to Summitville City Hospital Urgent Care to "just check things out" and "make sure everything was okay."

Reluctantly, it seemed, Patsy and Truman followed the EMT. Dane and Seth, as if in concert, moved closer. Another EMT, an older man with a shaved head and a powerful physique, pulled a gurney from the back of the ambulance.

Truman snapped, "I don't need that. I didn't jump, for Christ's sake."

The female EMT said, "It's just policy."

Truman stepped back, arms folding across his slight chest.

Patsy said, "Come on, honey, it'll be fun. How often do you get to take a ride in an ambulance?" She said it like she was talking about a spin on a Ferris wheel.

Truman, shaking his head, allowed the EMTs to help him aboard the gurney and lie down. He blew out a breath. "This is stupid."

Patsy said, "I'm coming with." It was not a question.

Dane and Seth watched as they loaded Truman into the ambulance. Patsy climbed in behind, and the EMTs slammed the double doors. They both jogged around to the front and drove away.

No siren.

The police were already gone.

Dane looked at Seth. "I can't go back inside."

Seth said, "You were very brave today."

Dane waved away the compliment. "You were the one. You really put your life on the line."

Seth thought for a moment. "So did you," he said. "So did you."

They said nothing as several moments ticked by.

At last Seth asked, "Should we maybe follow them down there? Make sure everything's good?"

"That's not a bad idea. My car's over here." Dane took his keys from his pocket and clicked the remote so that a beep issued forth from his Kia Soul.

"Just let me run and let Calhoun know what we're doing." Seth smiled.

Dane slapped his forehead. "Yeah! Thank goodness one of us is responsible and has a bit of common sense."

"Why, thank you. I don't think I've ever had those qualities attributed to me, so it means a lot." Seth grinned and winked at Dane.

As he stood alone in the parking lot, waiting for Seth to come back, Dane had a sudden realization. The realization, he thought, was a selfish one in light of what had just occurred, but there it was.

I just outed myself to the whole school today.

He shivered and didn't think it was because of the bitter wind.

What would happen now?

CHAPTER 9

SETH FOLLOWED Dane up the front steps of Summitville City Hospital. His thoughts were, he supposed, totally inappropriate for a caring teacher on a mission of mercy to a traumatized teenaged boy.

Dane Bernard is gay. I had no idea. Seth had been crushing on the man since he had seen him, only yesterday in the parking lot. The moment had been one of those instalove situations he read about in romance novels, the kind of thing he scoffed at, preferring more angst for characters as they struggled down the road to finding true love.

While he couldn't deny the immediate physical attraction toward the big man, he'd also sensed his caring and compassion. Dane Bernard was not only a very sexy specimen of the male species; he'd also proved himself to have a kind and caring heart.

What more could I ask for? Seth wondered. *Hot and sweet all rolled up into one delectable package. And gay too! Who knew?* Clarissa Bernard was in one of Seth's classes, and he'd just assumed her dad was straight, completely.

Seth's gaydar had failed him.

Dane turned to look down at Seth, who was frozen on the sidewalk at the foot of the stairs. He smiled. "Are you coming?" He held one of the heavy glass doors open for Seth. There was no indication on Dane's ruddy face that he had any idea of what was going through Seth's head.

"Sorry. Just got carried away with my thoughts." Seth hurried up the steps to join Dane.

"Understandable."

Seth looked back at Dane, coming in the door. "What?"

"It's understandable, I said. After the morning we've had…."

Seth felt heat rise to his face and laughed. "Oh! Right, of course."

Dane moved ahead toward the information desk in front of them. Seth stayed quiet, moored to his own internal dialogue. *He must think I'm a complete buffoon. Now come on, don't chastise yourself that way. You did a good thing this morning. Maybe even helped save a boy's life. That's what you need to concentrate on. The kid. The kid you just might be able to help even more if he'll let you.*

Seth moved quickly up behind Dane, listening as the bespectacled woman at the front desk told them Truman Reid was in room 402.

PATSY BRUSHED some hair away from Truman's forehead and gazed down at her son. He was sleepy now, his eyelids fluttering. The doctor who'd been in to see him had given him something to calm him and told Patsy that Truman would most likely fall asleep.

Her son's gaze met her own, and she liked to believe she could see gratitude there, that maybe Truman was comforted by the presence of his mom. Patsy hoped so, anyway. She prayed she wasn't part of the reason he had almost taken his life that morning.

She wanted to ask him so much, the foremost being: *Why?* She knew things were hard for Truman. Honestly, he was the biggest sissy she'd ever seen in her life, but he was *her* big sissy. And he couldn't help it, anyway. Truman had always been Truman, and she loved him for it. She wouldn't want him to be any different—more masculine—because then he'd no longer be himself. What kind of parent, Patsy wondered, would wish for their child to stop being himself?

That was crazy.

But she knew being as different as he was made things rough, made him the object of teasing and bullying. And she wished that could change. Patsy's heart clenched the way only a parent's can when they realize they can't be with their child every moment of life, protecting him from the cruelty it so generously and casually doled out.

Patsy was also angry. Didn't Truman think at all about how his suicide would affect her? How it would tear her apart?

Patsy didn't know if she could have gone on....

But she didn't want to think about a world without Truman in it. She didn't know if she was able to even imagine such a dark and lonely place.

She gazed down and watched as Truman drifted off. She was glad. Sleep offered oblivion, an escape from the pain even she hadn't known he was feeling. Oh sure, she realized he'd been teased and bullied, that he had no friends. Those things hurt her heart as much, if not more, she thought, than Truman's own. But Patsy had no idea how bad the pain had gotten. To want to end it all? That was nuts. *Why?* she asked herself once more. *Even if he has nothing else, he always has me.* She smiled. *And Odd. We're a little family unit. We don't have much in terms of material stuff, but we have each other. Isn't that enough? And besides, Truman's a smart kid. He'll leave this shit-hole town one day, go to one of those big cities like New York or Chicago, and be something. Then he can thumb his nose at those mean kids who tormented him. Why doesn't he see that? His whole life is still in front of him.* She placed a hand gently on his cheek. Truman smacked his lips and shifted a bit but did not wake.

Patsy wasn't sure what else she could do for him, other than continue to demonstrate her love and to make damn sure the kid knew that who he was and what he was were nothing to be ashamed of. And God help the person who tried to tell her different.

She allowed herself to finally sit in the blue vinyl-covered chair at the side of Truman's bed. He looked so tiny, the glare of the fluorescents making him look even paler than usual. All Patsy wanted to do was protect him. But the sad thing, and she knew this too, was that the older your kid got, the harder it was to shield him from life's cruelties.

The arrival of two men interrupted Patsy's thoughts. They were the teachers from Truman's school who had saved him. The first guy was Mr. Bernard, of course. And the second guy? He was a kind of geeky-looking fellow, with glasses, dark hair, and pale eyes. He wore a pair of jeans, button-down shirt, knitted tie, and a vest. She made him think of that Mr. Schuester on that show Truman used to love, *Glee.*

Patsy remembered being at PTA last fall and overhearing someone talking about how Mr. Bernard's wife had just been killed in a car accident. It was so sad! And him with two kids to raise alone!

The other guy had been with Truman when he came out of the school. Why, he must have been the one that pulled him back from the edge of that roof!

Patsy stood up, and her eyes welled with tears. "You guys!" she cried. "You guys are heroes!" She propelled herself first into Mr. Bernard's arms, squeezing him tight, and then moved on to the other guy. She couldn't help herself—the tension and the possibility of loss were too real. She sobbed into both of the men's chests, wetting their shirts.

Finally she pulled away, embarrassed. She dabbed with her fingertips at their damp shirts. "I'm so sorry. It's just that it's been so upsetting today! And if you guys weren't there to help, I might be at the damn morgue instead of here!" Patsy realized how awful she must sound, how stupid, with her hiccupping sobs and curse words. "I'm sorry," she said again weakly, trying to rein in her tears.

"No need to be sorry, Mrs. Reid," Mr. Bernard said.

Patsy smiled. "It's Ms. But you can call me Patsy. Everybody does. Down at the Elite Diner, I wear it on a little pin." She tried to laugh.

Dane said, "I'm Truman's English teacher. He's a bright kid, has great sensitivity, which I suspect works against him a lot."

"Oh yeah, you got that right." Patsy smiled. She wanted to make a good impression. She held out her hand to the younger guy. "Patsy," she said, looking into his eyes and noticing how they seemed to shift in color in the light, from green to brown.

"Seth Wolcott. I haven't had the chance to work with Truman in the classroom yet, but Dane told me in the car on the way over that he really has something. He writes beautiful short stories."

"And poems too! You should see the one he made up for me for Mother's Day." Patsy bit her lip and had to stop speaking for a moment. "It didn't rhyme, but it touched me here." She placed a hand over her heart.

"How's he doing?" Dane asked, looking over Patsy's head toward Truman.

"They gave him something—Valium, I think—to calm him down. Knocked him right out."

"Probably for the best," Dane said.

At his voice, Truman stirred a little.

Dane said, "Maybe we shouldn't be talking around him. Let him sleep. Can Seth and I treat you to a cup of coffee? We passed a Starbucks on the ground floor."

"Oh, I don't want to leave him." Patsy looked anxiously back at the bed. "But I also don't want to wake him up. You guys go get coffee if you want. I'll be here."

Seth smiled. "Tell you what. We'll go get us all something, and we'll bring it back. Then maybe we can talk a little just outside the room. Would that be okay?"

Patsy nodded.

Dane asked, "Do you want anything special? Cappuccino? Latte? Something to eat, maybe?"

"Aw, that's nice of you, but I'm just a plain old drip coffee girl. That's why I never go in a Starbucks. They make me scared I'll order wrong. Just coffee, black, for me."

"Coming right up."

Patsy watched the two men walk away.

When they got back a few minutes later, she stood from her chair and thanked them for the coffee. She followed them into the hallway.

She sipped. The coffee was too hot, so she just held it. It also tasted too strong, kind of burned. It wasn't like what they served at the diner.

The three of them stood in silence for a while. Patsy wasn't sure what to say. Finally she blurted out, "I'm worried."

"Of course you are," Seth said. "But Truman will get the help he needs."

"I talked to one of the doctors in the ER," Patsy said. "And he told me they're gonna transfer Truman up to Pittsburgh, to a hospital that has a psych ward, so he can be evaluated."

Dane nodded. "I think that's pretty common in cases like this. That way they can figure out what the boy needs, come up with a treatment plan."

Dane smiled at her, and she knew he meant to be reassuring, but all she felt was scared.

"What he did this morning, that's a serious cry for help."

She burst into tears again. She couldn't help it. How could she pay for all this? She had crappy insurance down at the diner.

Dane put his arm around her.

"I don't mean to sound like a bad mom or anything, but I don't know if my insurance will cover this stuff."

She watched as Dane and Seth exchanged glances. Seth said, "Why don't you let me go down to the offices and see what I can find out for you? You might be worrying for nothing. Lots of health plans cover psych—" He stopped himself. "Help for people like Truman."

"You don't think they'd try to change him, do you?"

"No. No, of course not," Seth said. "Do you have an insurance card with you?"

"Yeah." Patsy turned and went back into the room. She'd left her purse on the floor by Truman's bed. She fished out the card and handed it to Seth. "This is awful sweet of you. I hope you find out something good!"

He took the card. "I'll be right back."

Silently, Patsy watched as he walked away. "A nice man," she said. "You guys are going above and beyond. Hey, don't you need to be at school?"

"After what happened today, I doubt they'll get much done. The principal gave us permission to come down here, make sure Truman was okay."

"Oh, he's far from okay. We both know that." Patsy could feel another wave of tears coming on, but she stifled them. She needed to be strong for her boy. Besides, she didn't want these guys thinking she was a basket case. She shook her head and lowered her voice to just above a whisper. "As bad as this morning was, I'm still not completely shocked, you know? My heart aches for Truman. He's so lonely. He never has friends over. No one ever calls or comes around. Always by himself with his head in the clouds." She smiled. "Or his nose in a book. I swear that boy lives in his imagination." She went quiet as she remembered a little boy in his bedroom, way before all the teasing and bullying started at school, putting on shows. He'd stand on his bed and sing, and then jump to the floor and dance. He was pretty good too, for a little guy. His favorite was "Somewhere over the Rainbow" from *The Wizard of Oz*. It broke her heart to think of it. Even back then, he was alone. But at least it seemed like Patsy was enough company for him.

"I know," Dane said. "I've tried to talk to him some over the school year. It seems like he gets picked on almost every day." Dane shook his head. "It's terrible. I wish I could do more to help."

"Oh my! I heard some of what you said today. You do a lot, Dane, a lot. But my boy… I don't know." Her voice went even lower, and she knew it was barely a raspy whisper as she admitted, "I think he hates himself."

Dane squeezed her shoulder. "That might be true. And we need to change that."

"Oh, honey, I've tried. I don't have nothin' against gay people. And I've never made Truman feel he was nothing less than fabulous. Isn't that the right word?" She grinned.

Dane grinned back. "Yeah, that's the right word."

"But nothin' I say or do seems to make a difference. He just gets quieter and quieter, like he's in his own little world."

Dane nodded.

Seth came back.

Patsy breathed a sigh of relief. This talk with Dane was getting too hard for her right now. She appreciated his kindness, but she was so tired, all of a sudden. She smiled at Seth. "What did you find out?"

"Well, I got good news and bad news." He didn't ask her which one she wanted first, just plowed onward. "The good news is that Truman's stay here and at the hospital in Pittsburgh for evaluation will be covered by your insurance, after the deductible and co-pay."

"And the bad?"

Seth frowned. "I'm afraid your carrier doesn't cover ongoing therapy." He shrugged. "It sucks, but I thought you should know."

Patsy crumpled a little and leaned against the wall. "Figures. I don't know what I'll do. How can I help him? I can't afford to send him to a therapist."

Dane offered, "There are clinics with sliding scales, I believe."

"I doubt if there's anything like that here in Summitville."

Again she watched the two men exchange glances. She didn't want to hear any more from them. They would offer her all kinds of help that wouldn't be practical. In the end, though, she knew it would all rest on her shoulders to try to make things right.

It always had. She sighed. "Listen, guys, did you hear that?"

Dane shook his head, and Seth looked blank.

Patsy lied, "I think I hear him waking up." She smiled. "Thanks a lot for coming down here, but I need to go be with my boy."

"Are you sure?" Seth asked. "We can discuss some options. There have to be some options."

Patsy smiled, but her heart was filled with sadness and dread. When you were as poor as she was, options, like most everything else, were always just out of reach. "Maybe later." She gave each of them a hug. "We can talk later."

And she hurried into Truman's room, not waiting for a response. She both hoped and dreaded the men would follow her into the room.

But they didn't.

CHAPTER 10

SETH LOOKED at Dane, feeling a little surprised at her abrupt departure.

"Do you think she's okay?" he asked.

"Of course she's not okay," Dane said softly, voice pitched just above a whisper. "Her son just tried to kill himself."

Dane's face looked anguished, and Seth's heart went out to him. The way he cared for these kids was beyond admirable, not something Seth had seen a lot in his short career as an educator.

"I know. Stupid question."

"C'mon." Dane grabbed Seth's arm and led him away from the room. Seth figured he didn't want Patsy to hear them talking. They were silent in the elevator, through the hospital lobby, and on into the parking lot. During that whole time, Dane never removed his hand, gently clutching, from Seth's arm.

Seth liked it.

Outside, the wind was no less bitter, although the sun was higher in the sky. A light snow had begun to fall, and the sky was a mix of puffy dark gray clouds and blue sky, making shadows come and go on the pavement.

Dane took his hand away from Seth's arm and looked down at his hand, as though surprised. Seth wondered if he even realized he'd been holding on to Seth. Dane smiled and then glanced down at his watch.

"Wow."

"What?"

"It's only eleven o'clock. It seems like a whole day has already passed."

"I know."

Dane cocked his head. "Maybe you and I could go grab a burger before we head back? Talk about helping Truman, if you're on board for that."

"Of course I'm on board! The poor guy. I'd love to be able to help him. And lunch sounds like a very good idea. I didn't have any breakfast this morning, and I'm feeling a little depleted."

"You been to the Elite?"

"That's the diner where Truman's mom works, right?"

Dane nodded.

"Nah. Haven't had the chance yet."

Dane cuffed him gently on the back of the head. "Kid, you don't know what you're missing."

THE ELITE Diner was a throwback, but not in some ironic, retro way. It had all the things a "retro" diner in Chicago would include, Seth thought, yet he could tell immediately that the diner had stood here in Summitville's downtown for many decades. It was housed in a building made to look like an old railway car. Inside, the walls were quilted aluminum, and the floors were a scuffed and chipped checkerboard of red and gray linoleum. Unlike a "nostalgic" diner in Chicago, though, nothing here seemed new. Everything about it had the patina of years of use. The soda fountain spouts were tarnished. The wall above the big grill was stained from years of grease spatters. The counter, gray Formica, still looked good, but the glass cases, one with doughnuts and the other with what looked like a pumpkin pie, were dull, probably from all the grease in the air. The stools lined up at the counter were outfitted in sparkling red vinyl, but they too had seen better days. Many were patched with duct tape. Seth smiled. The smells—french fries, burgers—were comforting. "Great place," he said and meant it.

"You guys can sit wherever you like." A tired waitress, with hips that strained the polyester of her pink uniform and an upsweep of dyed red hair, gestured to the narrow confines.

"I see a booth open at the back. Let's take that. We'll have privacy." He grinned at Seth over his shoulder as he headed back to the booth. "Small town, but big ears."

Once they were settled in and had ordered—cheeseburger and fries for Seth and a hot meat loaf sandwich with a side of "wet" fries for Dane—they looked at each other, and Seth could feel the weight of the morning beginning to seep in. This was no first date.

Endora, no kidding, was their waitress's name. Before they could even start talking, she came back to the table.

"You guys want drinks with your meals? A shake maybe? Pop?"

Dane said, "We gotta have cherry Cokes. They're awesome. They still make them with fountain Coke and syrup. You'll die."

Or at least get early-onset diabetes, Seth thought, *from all that sugar!* "Sounds delicious." He smiled at Endora and said, "Conjure us up a couple of those!" and snickered.

Endora didn't get the magical reference. She walked away.

Even though the diner was bustling with the lunchtime crowd, it felt to Seth like there was a bubble of silence around Dane and him. He realized that they didn't really even know each other; they were just a couple of men thrown together by circumstance. He blurted out, "You were very brave today."

"Ah." Dane waved the compliment away. "You said that already. I just did my job. Tried to help a kid in need. You were the one. You could have both gone over that ledge." Dane shivered. "I get chills when I think about it."

Seth wanted Dane to know about their so-far-unspoken common ground. "Yeah, Truman. We worked together to help him, didn't we? We did a good thing, but I expect we still need to do a lot of work to make sure that kid doesn't pull something like that again." Seth was quiet for a moment. "But when I said you were brave, I meant something else."

He watched Dane go a little pale. A sickly smile spread across his face, which, oddly enough, didn't detract at all from the guy's magnetism.

"What? I don't understand."

Seth felt like he was putting a foot out to test the surface of an iced-over pond. Would it hold him? He swallowed and licked his lips. He kept his mouth shut as Endora brought their sodas, an honest-to-goodness red-and-white-striped paper straw sticking out of each fountain glass. Seth took a sip and had to admit the cold sweet was a revelation, no comparison to the stuff Coke put readymade into a can or two-liter bottle. He leaned forward. "Is that the first time you admitted to the school you were gay?"

Dane looked flustered. His eyebrows scrunched together. His gaze moved frantically all around the narrow confines of the diner, lighting restlessly on everything and nothing all at once. He too took a sip of the wondrous elixir they'd ordered, but he choked on his, his face reddening.

Finally his choking slowed to a few sputters. A couple of other diners turned to stare. Seth had gotten halfway up, ready to do the Heimlich if necessary.

But Dane composed himself. He laughed briefly. "Honest to God, today's the first day I ever told *anybody*, 'cept for my two kids." Dane grinned, but the sheepishness won out. "And that was only last night."

"Really?"

"Man, didn't you know? I was married for a long time—to a woman. And even that didn't end because of my being gay. It ended because she died, in a car wreck." Dane looked away for a moment. Wistful? Sad?

Dane chuckled again, but there was little mirth in it. "Hell, even I didn't know until after Katy—that was my wife's name—died." He paused, appearing to think. "I take that back. I knew. How can you not, right? You see a nice ass on a guy and your libido doesn't lie. But the difference, I guess, is you can refuse to *accept* what your eyes and your body—and sometimes your dreams—tell you. And that's where I've been my whole life, refusing to *accept* who I was." He sighed. "I guess I thought I could change."

"You can't change who you are," Seth said softly. "But you can change how you deal with it."

"I know that. Now. I just kept thinking that, if I played the part long enough and hard enough, I could become the man I was supposed to be." Dane stared down at the table.

Seth suddenly didn't know who needed his pity, his love, and his support more, Truman or Dane. He'd known closeted guys before, especially when he was first coming out and sought sexual experience in places like Chicago's lakefront parks and forest preserves. Many of the guys who showed up there were married men, coupled, he guessed, with unsuspecting women. Seth avoided them and held them in a certain amount of contempt.

Now, seeing Dane and how much he hurt, coming to grips with who he was, made Seth feel ashamed of his disdain for the married men he'd encountered in his past. He reached his hand out and covered Dane's with it.

Dane snatched his hand away and looked at him oddly. "What are you doing?" He seemed a little desperate.

"I just wanted to offer you some comfort. Coming out is hard. I didn't know today was your coming-out day." Seth decided now would be a good time to share with Dane, to let him know he was not alone. "I remember my own coming out. I was a senior in high school. I got Mom and Dad together in our living room and told them I had an announcement. I told them I'd just found out I had brain cancer and had three months to live."

"What?"

Seth laughed. "And then I told them I was kidding. I was just gay." He grinned. "They were so relieved. We never went through any of the angst some of my friends experienced. I never had to endure their horror stories. My folks were loving, accepting."

"So?" Dane wondered. "Your life has been—what? Easy?"

"Oh, I wouldn't say that. Is life easy for any of us? Really? But at least I never had the burden of carrying around a secret like you did. Man, that had to have been hard. Did you ever... act on your feelings?"

Dane's eyes glistened for a second, and he drew in a breath. "No," he whispered, his voice hoarse. Then he pulled himself together. Seth was surprised at how quickly Dane's mood changed, like a cloud moving over the sun, then away again. "Hard doesn't begin to describe it. So you're gay, huh? I would never have guessed." Dane scratched the back of his head.

Just then Endora arrived with their food. They grew quiet as she set down the plates and bottles of ketchup and mustard. She ripped off their checks and set them beside the food.

"No rush, sweeties. Just pay up front when you're done. Holler if you need anything."

She walked away. Seth returned his gaze to Dane. "You're surprised? Why?" he asked, biting into his cheeseburger.

"You just don't seem the type."

"What's the type?"

Dane wasn't touching his food. "Oh, c'mon. Like Truman," he said softly. "That kid couldn't hide it if he tried. I would imagine a young Truman Capote was very much like our Truman. It's kind of ironic that's his name." Dane smiled sadly.

Seth stuffed a couple of fries in his mouth. They were hand cut, skin on, and delicious. "*You're* not like Truman. At least not in the obvious way. So… why would you be surprised that I'm gay?"

Dane appeared to ponder the question for a while. "I guess, uh, I just kind of thought gay men were obvious. The only one I really know of, besides Truman and now *you*"—he grinned—"is Jimmy Dale, who has his own beauty parlor a couple doors down from here and who's been doing the ladies' hair here since my own mother was a girl. He has rings on every finger, a big dyed pompadour, and wears mascara and rouge. Sort of a poor man's Liberace." Dane burst out laughing. "I guess it was Jimmy Dale who allowed me to hold on to the belief that I couldn't be gay because I was nothing like him."

"You thought all gay men were effeminate? And you were the odd exception to the rule?"

Dane nodded.

Seth felt taken aback. Here was a rare creature in front of him—a twenty-first-century gay male with no real exposure to the gay community. Seth had come up and out in Chicago, with Pride marches and rallies, dozens of gay bars, sports leagues, gay newspapers. Hell, even the main street of the gayborhood—Halsted—was lined with rainbow pylons. "You haven't known many gay people, have you? Or let me rephrase that. You haven't known many people you knew were gay? I mean, you probably think you, me, Truman, and that Jimmy Dale fella are the only ones in town."

"Yeah, I guess." Dane cut a forkful of meat loaf and popped it in his mouth.

"The truth is, Dane, even in a small town like Summitville, there are probably dozens of gay people all around you. They just don't announce it, because here is maybe a little bit more backward than the big cities."

"A little bit?" Dane snorted.

"My point is this. I've known a ton of gay people, and the vast majority of them—by and large—are *not* people like Jimmy Dale. Not that there's anything wrong with being a little soft, veering a little more to the feminine side. Those guys, the ones I've known anyway, are actually tough sons of bitches, because they have such a hard lot and get beat up on, both literally and metaphorically, most of their lives." Seth grinned. "Try messing with any drag queen. You'll see." Seth grabbed a couple of fries and made them disappear. "But yeah, most of us are pretty everyday, pretty ordinary, just leading our lives. I know you think, right now, being gay is awful special, freakish even, but I'm here to tell you that it's just a variation on the human theme. And that's what we all are—human." He touched Dane's hand again and again was met with the same response. Seth frowned. He assumed Dane didn't want anyone in the diner to see the two men touching.

He'd have to work on that, because he most assuredly wanted to touch Dane some more. He took a sip of his Coke and decided to move on. "You said maybe we could help Truman? What would that look like to you?" Seth wondered if any attempt the two of them made to help Truman would also be helping Dane. He felt a small rush of pleasure and was suddenly glad fate—and a cheating lover—had brought him to this small town.

"I don't know," Dane said. "I guess it crossed my mind that we could maybe informally counsel the kid." He grinned, but the rapid shifting of his gaze told Seth that Dane was nervous. "I know I mentioned clinics with sliding scales that Patsy could take Truman to, and they do exist. But not here in Summitville. They're a good drive away. And I just worry that, because they're impractical, not to mention probably overloaded, it might be hard for Truman and Patsy to follow through."

"And that's where we'd come in?" Seth asked. "I don't have any training at all in counseling."

"Neither do I," said Dane. "But I think we both have one quality that any good therapist would have, should have—compassion."

"And we both know what's it's like to be gay." Seth put a hand on his chest. "An old, tired veteran of the homo wars." Then he pointed to Dane. "And a new recruit."

"I don't know if I've exactly been 'recruited,'" Dane said. "I mean, it's *not* a choice."

Seth burst out laughing. "You've learned the first lesson in Gay 101." He looked into Dane's eyes, noticing how icy and pale blue they were. It nearly took his breath away. "Anyway, it was just a figure of speech. How about if we call you a newbie instead?"

"I don't know if I'm 'new' to anything."

Seth rolled his eyes. "C'mon, man!" He slapped the table, grinning. "Lighten up. Can't I catch a break?"

Dane smiled back, thankfully. He shoved his plate away from him. It almost looked as though it had been licked clean. "I can talk to Patsy. How would you wanna do this?"

"I don't think it should be done on campus. Let's keep things casual, maybe see if we could drop by the house once a week or something. Just to talk and let him know that he's okay, because we are." Seth started to reach out to touch Dane's hand once more, then thought better of it and pulled back.

"Good thinking. Of course this all depends on Patsy and, naturally, Truman. They have to be on board."

"Oh, I think they will be." Seth smiled at Dane. "You know, this has been an awful morning, but in a perverse way, I'm kind of glad of it."

Dane cocked his head, but he was smiling. "Oh?"

"Yeah, because I got to know you better. And it looks like there's a bit of an opportunity to get even better acquainted." Seth could do this thing—raise one eyebrow independently of the other. He did it now. "I like you, Dane."

Dane looked around nervously. Seth thought he was probably checking to see if anyone had heard. In Summitville it was a dangerous thing, Seth guessed, for one man to say he liked another. God, what would happen if one said he loved him? Would a lightning bolt streak from the sky?

Love, Seth thought. *Let's not get ahead of ourselves here.*

Dane asked, "Are you sure you have time for this? I mean, it might go nowhere, but it might also go *somewhere*, and that could mean a real time commitment outside school."

"Dude, I just moved here from Chicago. I don't know anyone. Other than the obvious benefit of maybe doing some good in the world and helping a kid in need, I'm also hungry for something to do. Do *you* have the time? You're the one with two kids." Seth started to add "that you're raising alone" and decided against it.

"I'll make the time." Dane glanced down at his watch. "Shit. It's after noon. We need to hightail it back. I'll talk to Patsy after school." He leaned forward to grope in his back pocket.

Seth grabbed both checks off the table. "No. It's on me today."

Dane looked puzzled. "Why?"

"Because next time, buddy, you buy. This is my way of making sure there *is* a next time. I know you're a man of honor." Seth got up without waiting for Dane to argue.

CHAPTER 11

TRUMAN WAS silent on the way home from Pittsburgh. Patsy didn't want to pry, but she was curious about the three days he'd spent in the hospital's psychiatric ward. When she drove up to bring him home, one of the doctors, a man who looked not much older than Truman himself, had met with her, advising her that Truman should get ongoing therapy, that he needed to come to learn to accept himself. He'd said a bunch of other things too, but Patsy knew that, ultimately, whether or not Truman got well would depend on her.

It always did.

They drove west on a two-lane road bordered by naked trees whose branches looked like fingers reaching up to the curdled-milk sky. The outdoors was as bleak as Patsy's mood. The sky was gray, oppressive. It seemed the clouds pressed down on their noisy little car. Snow was imminent, and a few warning flakes danced in the air now and then. Patsy prayed she'd make it back to the house before any real snowfall began. Her tires were nearly bald, and icy roads were more of a threat to her than the average driver.

Once they got home, Patsy led the still-silent Truman to his room. "Why don't you lie down? You hungry? It's almost lunchtime. I can heat you up a can of chicken noodle. I can fix you a sandwich. We still have some of that deviled ham, and I think there's some of the swiss you like in there. Sound good?" She watched as Truman flung himself onto the bed. He turned away so he faced the wall.

Patsy wanted to scream. She wanted to cry. She wanted to go over and lie down on the bed with him and spoon, like when he was a little boy. It tugged at her heart, though, the realization that he was *not* her little boy, not anymore. That little boy might as well have died. He wouldn't be coming back around.

The young man on the bed seemed like a bit of a stranger. "Truman, honey? You wanna eat?"

"Yeah, sure. Whatever."

Patsy turned and started from the room. That teacher, Dane Bernard, had come over and talked to her a couple of days ago, when all the shit had gone down, and told her that he and that other teacher—Patsy couldn't remember his name—wanted to help. If it was okay with her, they'd like to come and hang out with Truman, maybe once a week or so, and see if perhaps they could help him grow to become a little more accepting of himself. To be happier.

Of course it was okay with her. Patsy would take any help she could get. And the price was right. Her mom had always said, "Honey, if it's free, you take it."

They said they'd come for the first time tomorrow, and Patsy realized she was pinning a lot of hope on these two guys. If nothing else, maybe they'd make Truman see he wasn't so alone in the world.

She was halfway to the kitchen before she stopped herself. "No," she said out loud. She turned and went back to Truman's room. She tiptoed to the bed, thinking maybe he'd fallen asleep. Odd was curled up at his feet on the foot of the bed. But when she peered over his shoulder, she saw his eyes were open, staring listlessly at the pale yellow wall in front of him.

Patsy sat down gently on the edge of the bed. Tentatively she reached out a hand and laid it on his back. When he didn't resist, she began rubbing with a gentle, circular motion.

"It's gonna be okay," she said softly.

"Sure, Mom. Whatever you say." His voice was dull, lifeless.

"Truman, honey, please don't be this way."

"How do you want me to be, Mom?"

He rolled over and sat up suddenly. He plastered a big fake grin on his face. It scared her.

"Is this how you want me to be?"

Truman slumped back down and resumed staring at the wall.

"Stop it." It hurt her to see him like this—her sweet boy robbed of his gentle heart.

"Go make the chicken soup, okay? I know you mean well. I just feel like crap. Besides, don't you have work?"

"Endora traded shifts with me. I have the whole day off now. But I do have to go in for Sunday breakfast and lunch."

She started to get up, but something unfinished hung in the air, almost like a bad smell. They had never really talked, not really, not beyond the simple stuff like how Truman was sleeping in the hospital, what he'd eaten for lunch, stuff like that. She went back and—damn it—went ahead and did what every common sense impulse told her was wrong and inappropriate.

She lay down beside Truman.

But it felt right. She wrapped her arms around him and pulled him close to her chest. "Is this okay?" she asked, her voice a little shaky, unsure.

He didn't say anything for a minute, and Patsy thought maybe she should just back off. Then she heard him sniffle. He trembled a little, and Patsy knew he was crying.

"It's okay, Mom," he managed to get out. "It's nice." His voice was breathless, a little raspy.

Patsy lay still, staring at the back of her son's head. When had his blond hair, always so downy and fine, become coarser? When had it darkened? It used to be almost white. "Why, honey?"

Truman didn't say anything for a long time, long enough for Patsy to wonder if she'd heard him. Finally, though, he found his voice.

"Because no one's ever gonna love me."

"Oh, baby, I love you. With all my heart. You'll always be my little man. Numero uno. And I love you just the way you are."

"I know, Mom. I love you too. But you have to." He drew in a shuddering breath. "But—oh crap, I might just as well say it—no guy's ever gonna love me. I'm a freak. Why was I made this way? Why couldn't I just be like other boys?"

Patsy hugged him tighter. "Why would you want to? You're wonderful, baby. You're a good young man. Smart. Handsome. You have nothing to be ashamed of."

"Again... mother speaking."

"Honey. Believe it or not, you won't always be this scared teenager living in your mom's house. You're gonna grow into a fine man and make me the proudest mother that's ever been. I don't hope for that. I know it. You're gay. So what?" Patsy shrugged. "Don't you know gay people can now get married—in every state? I'm gonna dance at your wedding one day. You're just as entitled to happiness as everyone else."

"You're sweet, Ma, but you don't know."

"Don't know what?"

Truman said nothing.

"Know what?" Patsy squeezed him a little tighter.

"There *was* someone. I thought he loved me." Truman continued to talk—to the wall. "We were together, you know? In that way."

Patsy swallowed. She had a bunch of questions. *Who? Where? When?*

"I thought he loved me, Mom. I thought maybe, one day, he'd realize he was like me and we could be together."

A chill coursed through Patsy. Truman was only fourteen. Had someone abused her son?

"Who was it, Truman?"

"I don't want to say."

"Was it someone older?" A flame of rage ignited in Patsy's gut.

"Yeah."

"Who?"

"Only a little older, Mom. Don't get all bent out of shape. It wasn't Stranger Danger." Truman sniffed. "He's a senior." He turned to her so their noses were almost touching. "Can I tell you everything? Will you promise me you won't say a word about this to anyone, especially him?"

"I don't know if I can make that promise, sweetie."

He turned back to the wall. "Just forget it. Can you go heat up that soup now?"

Patsy was at a crossroads. She needed to know what Truman was keeping secret, what, in fact, maybe pushed him to the edge of that rooftop. But what if she made a promise she couldn't keep?

She had to take the chance. If she needed to talk to someone about whatever it was Truman would reveal, she'd do so only after persuading him it was the right thing to do. "I won't breathe a word to anyone. Just tell me."

"You know how I used to take those walks down by the river?"

Pasty said, "Yeah?" She remembered how, all summer, it became a habit of Truman's, around dusk, to take Odd out for a stroll. She thought nothing of it at the time. In fact, if she were being honest with herself, she was a little relieved to have them both out of her hair for a little while so she could nap. She was always so tired after being on her feet all day in the diner. She usually fell asleep with her head on the kitchen table with the TV blaring some reality show. Now that she thought about it, she seldom even remembered when Truman would come home from those outings. She felt a little ashamed. She should have been paying more attention.

"Well, when Odd and me would head down to the river, we used to meet the guy." Truman drew in a deep breath. "My guy. Or at least I thought he was."

"Truman, who was it?"

"Ma, that's not important."

"What is important, then?"

Truman sniffed again, and the next sentence emerged in a strangled voice. "That I loved him." He wept.

Patsy felt a little sick, but she drew even closer to her boy, hugging him hard. "That's wonderful."

"No!" The sobs and the tears dried up suddenly. "It's not wonderful, because it turned out he didn't love me back. He was just using me." He turned on his back and regarded Patsy out of the corner of his eye, as if weighing what he would say next. Finally, in a breathless rush, he let the words out. "For sex."

Patsy couldn't help it—she was no prude and had been around the block herself more times than she cared to admit—she shuddered. He was her baby! Just a little kid! Not even all the way grown! And he was having sex. "What did you do with him?" Patsy asked, a little breathless, not sure she could stand the response.

"Do you really want to know the specifics?"

Patsy gnawed for a moment at a hangnail on the edge of her thumb. "I guess not. But at least tell me this much—were you careful?"

"Good God, Mom. Yes. We were careful. We were both virgins anyway, so I don't think there was any need, but we used rubbers just the same."

Patsy wanted to be relieved. She wanted to congratulate Truman for having a good head on his shoulders, but all she could do was stare at the ceiling. She needed to deal with her son being sexual on her own time, she realized. Maybe later tonight, when she was by herself and in her own bed. The prospect was not that thrilling, though. She tried to shift the focus away from the carnal. "But you loved this guy?"

"Oh yeah, Mom! He was—is—so fine!" Truman got a little breathless. "I never thought someone like him would ever look twice at someone like me."

Patsy chastised, "Sweetie, *a lot* of people would look at you twice. Don't undersell yourself."

"But he was a jock, Mom. One of the most popular guys in school. He—" Truman stopped, probably realized he was saying too much. Summitville was a small town, and Patsy had a job that put her into contact, sooner or later, with almost everyone who lived there.

"Anyway, I was just a thing to him." Truman turned away again to stare at the wall. "A receptacle."

Patsy winced. It would have hurt no less if Truman had jabbed her with a knife. Funny how a single word could conjure up so much pain. But Patsy herself had been a "receptacle" in her own past and knew the pain and emptiness that went with it, especially when you thought you were in love with the person in question. Why couldn't she shield Truman from pain like this?

"Oh, honey." She rubbed his arm, touched his hair, and wished she knew the right words to say.

"I tried to let him know how much I cared about him the last time we were together, tried to let him know—just like you always tell me—that being gay was okay, nothing to be ashamed of." He stopped for a long while. "He laughed at me. Called me a fag, even though we'd been doing stuff with each other and to each other in secret for

89

months. And then he hit me. Punched me in the stomach." Truman swallowed. "So hard I threw up. He told me he never wanted to see me again, and that if I ever told anyone what we'd done together, no one would believe me and he'd hurt me a lot worse."

They were quiet for a long time. And it hurt Patsy, in her own gut, to think of Truman being treated that way. It made her furious. It made her heart ache.

At last Truman laughed, but it was a bitter laugh. "Hey, look at me, Ma. I'm *not* crying like some big old sissy boy. This is the part where I'm supposed to cry, right?"

Patsy just shook her head. Perhaps she'd shed enough tears for the both of them. Finally she said, "You feel what you feel, honey. Whatever it is, it's valid."

"You're so wise, Mom."

Patsy snorted. "Yeah, which is why I've got such a promising career and live in this mansion."

They both laughed.

"After that happened," Truman said, "that's when things went dark, when they seemed so hopeless." He looked at her again, then away. "That's when I decided to, um, decided to climb up on that roof."

Patsy wanted to say something then, to remind him there was always hope. She wondered if the ache that accompanied the mental image of Truman on that roof would ever leave her.

But Truman was three steps ahead. "Now that just seems like a jerk move. Cowardly. What a loser would do. That guy wasn't, isn't, worth it. Sure, he's all hot, but he's got no heart. What he doesn't know and I do, now, is that when he slugged me, he was slugging himself. He hates himself, and until he can turn that around, he'll never love anyone else." He smiled at Patsy and brushed one of *her* tears away with his thumb. "I'm better off without him."

"You are, sweetheart, you are. There's a boy out there somewhere who deserves a guy like you, and he's just waiting. Like you, he thinks he'll maybe never meet his Prince Charming, but you will turn up one day and turn his world upside down. I just know it."

It was Truman's turn to hug, and he did—hard. "Thanks, Mom," he said softly. "You have no idea how much it helped, just getting this out."

Patsy clung to him, not wanting to let go. It both heartened and saddened her, this little scene. On the one hand, it was wonderful that Truman was able to draw some conclusions about his own worth and to see he was better than this other boy. But he'd done it on his own. Patsy hadn't said anything that helped him. She was proud of him for that, but it also pained her. It was one more nail in the coffin of his childhood, and it made her realize that parenting was just one long process of letting go.

It broke her heart. It also broke her heart that the encouragement she *did* give him, about Prince Charming, rang so hollow in her own ears. She'd had such a wild and promiscuous past. She would have thought, through all those nights and all those men, one would emerge who would see beyond her big tits and party-girl willingness, who would see her kind and nurturing heart, but none ever had. And now, when she looked in the mirror in the morning before she put on any makeup, she witnessed the fading of her looks, and it made her wonder, seriously, if anyone would ever come to see her for what was real and good inside her.

Like Truman did.

Funny how the tables turned.

She realized Truman, unburdened, warm, had fallen asleep in her arms. She held him close, petting his hair gently, and softly hummed her special lullaby for him, "You Are My Sunshine."

No matter what the future held, he would always, on some level, be her baby.

CHAPTER 12

DANE TAPPED lightly on Clarissa's door and then opened it. "Punkin?"

She didn't look up. She had her earbuds plugged in, and her phone was next to her on the pillow, probably blasting out the latest Maroon 5 love song. She had her iPad open on her lap, and her fingers were flying over its surface. He cleared his throat and repeated himself. She glanced up, failing to hide the irritation on her face. She gave him a look that said "What?"

Dane looked down at the carpeting for a moment, trying to conceal his hurt. Since he had told her he was gay, she'd been distant, as if his revelation was a personal affront. Maybe it was. Maybe it was hard for her to get over her dad being a different man than she thought. But still, couldn't she cut him a little break? At least *try* to understand? *Try.* That's all he asked.

He stood there waiting, wringing his hands, in her bedroom doorway. Finally, she got the message and yanked the earbuds out. "I know. I know. It wasn't a choice. You didn't ask for any of this," she said, parroting back to him the different ways he'd attempted to explain to her his new sense of self, his acceptance.

"You're right, Clarissa." He sighed. "But I wasn't stopping by to tell you those things. I just wanted you to know I'm heading out for a couple of hours and I might not make it home in time for supper. There's deli ham and turkey, some swiss cheese, and that spelt bread you like in the fridge, so you guys can make sandwiches." He grinned. "And salt and vinegar potato chips," he added, like the snacks were pure gold.

"I hate those," Clarissa snapped.

"Probably because the last time you had them, you ate a whole bag and then barfed." Dane closed the door on his daughter before he could see her reaction. He felt bad, but he couldn't wipe the stupid grin off his face.

He headed downstairs, where Joey was in front of the TV, watching *Judge Judy*. She was telling some poor abashed defendant not to pee on her leg and tell her it was raining.

"*Judge Judy*? Really? *You* like that show? I had no clue." *Judge Judy* must be a recent development in his son's viewing habits. Dane didn't imagine teenage boys were the judge's target audience.

"Yeah. She's cool for an old lady. She tells it like it is. I like to watch her give these doofuses an earful. It tickles me."

Dane chuckled. "Well, it'd be cool if you'd watch something a little better for your brain—"

Joey cut him off. "Dad, it's training me to be an attorney."

"All righty, then." And Dane let it go. It did make a certain amount of sense. "Anyway, I'm heading out for a bit. Go ahead and eat if you're hungry." He repeated what was in the fridge and pantry, which made Joey pause the hatchet-faced judge in the middle of her latest diatribe and race for the kitchen.

Adolescent boys are so much easier. As Dane headed out the front door to meet Seth Wolcott for their first visit with Truman, he thought, *Maybe not.*

SETH WAITED outside the Reids' little house for him. He had his nose buried in his Kindle and didn't look up when Dane parked his car across the street. Dane pulled his key from the ignition and simply sat for a few moments regarding the young man across the street, telling him things he probably would never have the nerve to say in real life.

You are so good to be doing this. So many guys your age would be doing anything but. They'd be out living it up in a bar, or looking for hookups online, or whatever it is young gay men do these days. Dane found the prospect of Seth looking for hookups, either online or in the real world, was a depressing thought. Scratch that. He found the thought caused a completely irrational twinge of jealousy to emerge right there in his gut, where he could really feel it.

And he told himself, *You have no right to feel jealous. My God, the kid is at least ten, maybe fifteen years younger than you. And besides, you don't even know him. Not really. And another thing—you don't need to be thinking about guys, not yet. Not when Joey and Clarissa are still struggling with the idea of a gay dad. Not when you're still struggling with the idea of being gay yourself. Give yourself time. Maybe in ten, twenty years, you'll be ready for a more physical thing.* Dane chuckled at this last thought. And then another notion popped into his head. *But he sure is cute.*

As if he had heard Dane's assessment, Seth looked over at him. Dane hurried to get out of the car for fear of having been caught staring. His scalp tingled and heat rose to his cheeks. He was thankful it was winter and already growing dusky so his blush would be hidden.

He hurried over to Seth, a big grin plastered on his face. "What're you reading?"

"*The Fault in Our Stars.* I'm thinking about it for my college-prep lit class. Maybe next year."

"Good book," Dane said. "You ready for this?"

Seth's smile wavered. "I don't know. I mean, don't get me wrong. Nothing would make me happier than helping this poor kid out, but I'm not all that confident about my ability to do so. You know?"

"I know. But I think you're worrying too much about your lack of formal education. I know you have a good heart, and I think that counts for more than any degree."

"So sayeth the man who's been an educator for how many years?" Seth turned to follow Dane to the Reids' front door.

"I'd rather not say," Dane replied, hoping he didn't sound too coy. Hoping it wasn't too obvious that he wanted to minimize the difference in their ages.

Why should that matter?

Dane followed Seth up to the front door. He noticed how broad Seth's shoulders were, how thick and curly his hair was, and—damn it—how high and tight his ass rode. He wondered for a moment what it would feel like to bury his fingers in those curls. Or, better, to grab a handful of that ass and squeeze until the poor guy yelped. *These are not appropriate thoughts at all! Shame on you!*

So he said, to change the subject, "I didn't realize they were this bad off." The house looked like something a strong gust of wind or a rise of the Ohio River's current, a block away, could sweep off its foundation. The house seemed exhausted, as though it could collapse on itself back into the earth—with relief. He frowned as he saw how Patsy, or maybe Truman, had made an effort to block out winter's chill by tacking old dry cleaning bags across the windows for insulation. He noticed how the paint on the trim peeled, revealing rotting wood underneath. Patsy, or maybe Truman, had tried to perk up the gray and depressing exterior with a little plastic pot of fake red geraniums near the front door. The effect was heart wrenching.

The thought "poor Truman" had never been more literal.

But when Patsy flung open the front door, she couldn't have been more in contrast with the house's run-down exterior. She was vibrant, smiling, alive. Dane thought once again how young she looked—she could pass for early twenties. This afternoon she had on a pair of old jeans, ripped at the knees, and an oversized Ohio State sweatshirt hoodie, scarlet and gray. She was barefoot and looked like a child.

"Hey there," Dane called out, hurrying to catch up with Seth.

"Come on in, guys. I'm so glad you could make it. Truman will be too."

After they were settled in the cramped living room, Patsy closed the front door behind them. The place smelled like cooking grease and wet dog. Dane hoped it was something Truman and Patsy had gotten used to. The living room was a collection of mismatched thrift store furniture representing the 1970s and 1980s in particular. There was a teal vinyl-covered couch and matching recliner. Dime store framed floral prints decorated the walls, while along the top of a low bookshelf was arranged a row of framed photographs. They were all of Truman—a chronicle of his life from what looked like the day he was born practically up until today.

The TV was one of those with the picture tube in the back, and it looked big, black, and boxy. It was a relic to Dane, like those old refrigerators with the motors on top. At least it wasn't on.

"Take a seat. Can I get you somethin'? I just made a pot of coffee."

"That sounds great," Seth said. He sat on the couch.

Dane took the recliner.

Patsy called from the kitchen, "Truman'll be right back. He's taking Odd Thomas out for his after-supper walk."

"Odd Thomas?" Seth wondered. "After the Dean Koontz character?"

Dane nodded, but Patsy didn't say anything. They listened as she brought mugs down from the cupboard and poured coffee. "You guys like sugar? Cream? I got Coffee-mate."

"Just black for me," Dane said.

"I'll take lots of both," Seth said and grinned at Dane. He winked. "I like my coffee like I like my men."

"White?" Dane asked, horrified.

"No, silly! I meant sweet." He reached out to nudge Dane's foot with his own.

Patsy came in holding two steaming mugs aloft. Dane recognized the Fiesta ware; he had the same stuff in his own home. The pottery was just down the river, so almost everyone around here owned at least some Fiesta.

"That smells good." Dane accepted a mug from Patsy.

Once they were settled, Patsy said, "Truman's doing a lot better."

"Really?" Seth took a sip of his coffee. It must have pleased him because he smiled.

"Really. Him and me, we had a long talk last night. He opened up." Patsy smiled, shaking her head. "I don't know that he got it from me, but my kid's got a good head on his shoulders." Her smile widened. "I really think he's gonna be okay."

Dane didn't want to say that it was awfully soon after Truman's suicide attempt to be so optimistic, but he hoped she was right.

"You'll see when he gets back," Patsy said. "Sometimes just talking things out can help us see what we need, that things aren't as awful as we think."

Dane felt a pang. He wished that were true with Clarissa.

"Here he comes," Patsy said, excitement rising in her voice, as though this was a surprise party.

Dane looked up to see Truman's silhouette through the sheer curtains. A little dog trotted along ahead of him.

Patsy stood. "Damn that kid. If I've told him once, I've told him a thousand times, 'Don't let Odd off the leash,' but do you think he listens?" She turned back to them, Dane supposed, for support. "That dog's gonna get run over by a car if Truman's not careful!"

Seth just shrugged and said, "Kids."

Truman came inside, bringing with him a gust of bitter, almost Arctic wind. The little dog, Odd, rushed into the room. He circled around, almost chasing his own tail, yapping joyously. Then he got busy sniffing both men, pointed nose going from crotch to crotch.

Patsy raised her eyebrows. "See? Odd fits, don't it? Weirdest looking—and acting—dog I ever saw."

Seth laughed.

Dane patted his lap. "Come here, boy!"

Odd jumped into Dane's lap, licked his face, and finally settled in for whatever attention he could get. Dane began rubbing him behind the ears and petting him. If he stopped, the dog would nudge Dane's hand with his nose to get him to continue. The dog's presence made him remember talking with Katy last fall about getting the kids a puppy for Christmas, a plan he'd never seemed to be able to follow through on. Now he thought maybe it would be a good idea, a way to help them bond again.

Patsy stood. "I gotta get ready for work, unfortunately. Dinner shift. This is fried chicken night—all you can eat—and we get swamped." She sighed. "Great tips, though." She left the room.

Odd hopped down unceremoniously from Dane's lap and trotted after her. Dane watched the dog.

Truman said, "He's fickle like that. But he'll be back."

Truman looked different here than he did at school. Bigger somehow. Tonight he had on a pair of skinny jeans and a paisley-print button-down shirt. Around his neck he wore a bright scarlet scarf that picked up some of the red in the shirt. Dane thought it was clothes like these that got Truman into trouble. Maybe they could talk about that at some point. Perhaps Dane could even buy him some regular Levi's, a pair of sweatpants, a couple of T-shirts.

They were quiet for a while, and Dane thought it was because none of them knew what to say to break the ice. At least he didn't.

Finally Seth set down his coffee on an end table and leaned forward, his hands clasped between his knees. "So how are you doing, Truman? You feeling better?"

"Better than what?" Truman asked. He got up and went into the kitchen. They heard him rummaging around, doors opening and closing, the slap of the refrigerator as he shut it.

He returned with a bright orange Fiesta plate. On it he had laid out slices of American cheese and deli ham, cut into squares, and saltines. "A little somethin'," he said. "I don't know about you guys, but I'm starving." He set the plate on the coffee table, shoving a stack of *People* magazines over to make room.

The food was a distraction, Dane realized. But the three of them went at it with gusto, and in a few minutes, all that was left were crumbs.

Seth repeated his original question about how Truman was doing.

"Funny you should ask that," said Truman. "It's weird. A few days ago, if you'd told me I'd have a totally different outlook on life in general, I wouldn't have believed you. But last night, after breaking down and telling my mom all my secrets, getting everything off my chest, I felt so much better." He glanced over at Dane. "Remember when you said how we never know what's coming? How we can't predict anything from one day to the next?"

Dane nodded.

"You were right. I don't know why, but just letting go and opening up a little was like lifting this weight even I didn't know I was carrying around off my shoulders."

Dane nodded again, wishing he had some wise words of encouragement and validation to add, but all he could think of was how what Truman said about getting a weight off one's shoulders applied to him. Coming out—to both his kids and accidentally to the whole school—had let him breathe easier. And, except for Clarissa, the reaction had so far not been as big of a deal as he once imagined. The lack of interest from most people was almost disappointing.

Truman glanced down at the floor, rubbing at a cracker crumb in the shag carpeting with his bare toe. "The talking, and in this really weird way, the fool thing I did on the roof, really changed things." He chuckled but then looked serious again. "That last part? Whew. Never would have thought trying such a shitty loser move would have actually somehow made me feel better. But it did." He shrugged. "I guess it showed me how low I could sink and, more importantly, that people like you guys cared."

"That's great, Truman," Seth said softly. Dane looked over at Seth and could read the admiration Seth had for the boy in his features.

Truman sighed. "Tomorrow I'm going back to school."

He smiled again, but there was something so sad and wistful in that smile that Dane felt his heart clench.

"It's easy to pretend things are all cool when I'm here at home with Mom and you guys. But it'll be a whole 'nother story when I get back in the hallowed halls of good ole Summitville High." He looked at both of them in turn, then back down at the floor.

Seth leaned forward. "We'll be there, Truman. And no matter what, you can come to us for help any time you need it."

Dane said, "He's right. If anyone gives you a hard time, just let us know."

Truman grinned, but there was something bitter in the expression, like a fly in a bowl of honey. "I appreciate that. But I can't go running to you guys every time somebody calls me a fag or trips me in the hallway. Or punches me in the kidney in the lunch line." He barked out a short laugh that brought Odd Thomas out from Patsy's bedroom. "Oh yeah, all that and more have been part of the daily adventures of yours truly. Except now I don't go to lunch, so that kind of shut down the lunch line torture." He paused. "And I bet those guys really miss it."

Dane could see that Truman really dreaded going back to school—and with good reason. He wished there was something more he could do, like getting him into a private school in Pittsburgh or something. But even if he did that by some miracle, who's to say the teasing and the bullying would stop? It could just be the same script with different players, albeit more affluent ones. No, Dane knew, like he knew this fact for himself, that it wasn't what was outside that needed the help; it was what was inside.

We can't change the world—only our reaction to it. Truman needed to be strong, somehow, in his own self-worth to truly combat the fear and hatred he encountered far too often for a boy his age—for a person of any age, really.

Seth, of course, proved to be the wiser of the two of them, and he said what Dane was thinking. "Listen, buddy, when I first came out, I thought the whole world was gonna be against me. But you know what? It was incredibly freeing. For one thing, being honest showed me that not as many people as I thought were against me or, in fact, that they even cared. Most people, I think you'll find, are too busy dealing with their own crap to be as concerned with yours as you might think." He blew out a breath. "And the ones that had a problem with it? You know what I said to myself about them?"

Truman leaned forward, eager to know. Dane leaned forward too.

"I said, and you'll pardon this and promise me you understand that I'd never say this in the classroom, but I said...." He paused for a moment, for effect maybe. "I said, 'fuck 'em.' If they couldn't accept me or didn't like me for who I was, for something that was really unchangeable and real about me, then fuck 'em. They didn't deserve to know me. And their problem—which was being afraid, because really that's what all hate's rooted in—was not mine." He sat back, presumably to let the words sink in.

Truman grinned. "That's a great attitude. It's easier said than done, though."

Seth shook his head. "No. You can't cop out like that. You can't change anyone else. But you can change *you.*" Seth stood and lightly touched Truman's chest with his finger. "You need to know, as I know your mom has told you and we're here to tell you today, that you're okay. There. Is. Nothing. Wrong. With. You. You have lots of great attributes, and I'm sure, just like everyone else on the planet, you have some bad characteristics. But just being who you are, who the Lord made, is *not* one of those bad characteristics. Bud, you need to hold your head up high, banish any shame, and let the world know you're one of God's children and they need to be okay with that. And if not?"

Truman said, "Fuck 'em."

Both Dane and Seth couldn't contain their smiles. And Dane couldn't contain the feelings Seth stirred up inside. He was certain his fellow teacher had no idea Dane was soaking up his words like a sponge, appreciating them, absorbing them, filing them away for later, darker hours. Yes, this time was supposed to be for Truman and his healing, but there was nothing wrong, was there, if Dane got something out of it too? In many ways, he and Truman were on the same level, developmentally speaking.

"That's right," Seth said. "You're a fast learner."

"Putting it into practice, though, might be a little harder than it sounds."

Seth nodded. "Don't be so negative, kid. Yeah, you're right. It's not easy. What is? The teasing and the bullying won't stop. But if you, slowly but surely, do change who you are and how you react to it, *on the inside*, you'll be so much further ahead. Because once you love who you are, really love him, warts and all, the 'slings and arrows of outrageous fortune' become a lot easier to bear."

"Shakespeare," Truman murmured.

"Very good!" Seth cried. "What play, though?"

"Hamlet." Truman grinned.

Seth nudged Dane. "This kid is going places."

Dane nodded. He felt strange. He wanted, suddenly, to go off and be by himself, to think about the things Seth had said, to "absorb" them. He realized his own coming-out process wouldn't be complete until he loved himself—and he didn't know if he did, not yet. He carried around so much guilt about all the years he'd worn a mask and the secrets he'd kept from those who loved him. And then there was Katy—surprisingly Katy. She was no longer even with them, but he still experienced her presence. He just didn't feel anything in regards to what she would think about him and the truth he'd kept concealed from her through all the years of their marriage.

"He sure is," Dane forced himself to say. He realized he hadn't been doing much to allay the boy's pain, to make him more confident about facing that first day back at school, and thought that maybe now would be a good moment to offer the kid some advice, while at the same time forcing his mind away from himself and his own struggles. So he returned to a thought he'd had earlier and uttered something he thought would be helpful.

"And Truman? Can I give you some advice about when you return to school tomorrow? I don't want you to take this the wrong way. I want you to know I'm only saying this out of love and wanting you to fit in."

He glanced over at Seth, whose eyebrows had come together questioningly.

"The way you dress? The pride T-shirts and—" Dane cut himself off to gesture up and down at Truman's person. "—that getup you have on right now. They're kind of screaming to the world you're gay. And I think that makes you more vulnerable, more of a target. Now maybe if you just wore some jeans and a T-shirt, maybe some Chucks, you might not open yourself up to so much to bullying." Dane smiled and tried to put caring and benevolence into the expression. Since that first day, when Truman had worn that "It Gets Better" T-shirt with its rainbow flag, Dane had thought the boy courted some of his own trouble.

He glanced over at Seth, expecting a smile or some words of agreement.

But he didn't get what he expected.

What he got was an open-mouthed stare from Seth. Truman had shut down, and his gaze hovered somewhere above Dane's head.

Had he said the wrong thing? He was just trying to help the boy fit in! Help him not stick out so much as a target. Was there something wrong with that?

Apparently there was. Seth didn't say anything for a while, and when he did, he began with a glance at Dane, sending a weak smile in his direction. He scratched his head and soon turned back to Truman.

"Listen, Mr. Bernard here means well."

He glanced nervously at Dane again, who wanted to ask "What did I say? What did I say?"

"But I have to disagree with him." He smiled at Dane, begging with those incredible hazel eyes—for what? Forgiveness? Understanding? "See, Truman, being yourself is all about holding your head up and telling the world you're proud of who you are. You shouldn't hide that. You shouldn't dress a certain way to fit in if it's not you. You shouldn't try to change the way you talk or the way you walk because you think it'll make you less of a target and, I might add, just like everyone else." He leaned close to Truman and put a hand on his knee. "You should celebrate who you are. Be proud of the differences. Now, I don't like to deal in 'shoulds,' but that's one I think bears saying. Who you are is unique. Special. Don't hide it. Don't dress it down because you think some narrow-minded fool doesn't get you."

Dane silently peered at his own clothes—his Oxford-cloth button-down, his khakis, and his Asics running shoes. "Should I dress differently?" he wondered, realizing too late he was speaking out loud. This wasn't about him! But in a way it was, in more ways than Dane expected. Still, he shouldn't be asking such things, not with Truman sitting between them. "Never mind," he said quickly.

Dane looked to Seth and nodded. "Mr. Wolcott here is right. He's absolutely right. Forget what I said. I'm still learning. Be yourself. Be proud."

Dane didn't really recall much of what else they said. He did know it was more of the same: encouragement, the speaking of support and of being available to Truman.

By the time they left, Dane felt himself oddly shaken.

OUTSIDE, SETH said, "I'm sorry if I made you feel bad."

Night had fallen, and with it, the temperature had dipped. Dane shivered and rubbed his hands together, blew into them for warmth. "Oh, you didn't."

Seth put a hand on his shoulder. "Oh, but I did."

Dane stopped and stared at him. "Maybe a little. Is how I dress so bad?"

Seth laughed. "You know what? I think you missed my point. Gay people come in all different shapes and sizes. We all dress different ways. We like different movies, books, TV shows, music. Everyone who doesn't know any gay people—or rather, *think* they don't know gay people—wants to stereotype. Depending on who we are, they want to put us in drag, in leather, in flannel and work boots. You dress just fine *for you*."

Seth looked him up and down, and in that look, which lasted so long it made Dane feel a little giddy, Dane read appreciation.

Or at least hoped he did.

His guess was confirmed when Seth finished up by saying, "You, sir, look just fine. *Very* fine. Just the way you are."

They went quiet after that. Dane felt a little embarrassed. He'd never in his life known how to graciously take a compliment, and especially not one from another man. The guy he saw in the mirror every day was a big, lumbering oaf. Sort of the like a Lennie from *Of Mice and Men*, except a Lennie with brains and an English degree. That Seth saw something different was intriguing, scary, and—exciting.

"It's fucking freezing out here. It must be in the single digits." Seth's gaze met Dane's in the darkness, which had now fallen completely. "Do you wanna go grab a bite somewhere? The lunch meat, cheese, and crackers didn't quite do it for me."

Dane thought of his kids at home, eating lunchmeat and cheese, and wondered whether he should just beg off. He was torn. He knew that if he went home, Joey would still be glued to the TV, and Clarissa would most likely continue to pretend he didn't exist. They probably both would have already made themselves something to eat. In fact, Joey was already tearing into the food when Dane left the house.

Or… he could go have dinner with this handsome young man who was asking him. Of course, it wasn't a date, and Dane reminded himself that Seth was most likely simply hungry. *We all have to eat….*

"Why not?" Dane said. "Let me just call my kids." He pulled his phone from his pocket and rang Joey's cell. His son assured him that they'd eaten, homework had been done, and Joey was now watching an episode of *Orange is the New Black* on Netflix. Clarissa had gone to her friend Jerri Lynn's house down the street, where she was once again spending the night. Dane couldn't say anything about that—not now. But he could object to his twelve-year-old son's viewing habits.

"I told you, Joey. You're too young for that show."

"Yeah, Dad. Whatever. I'll turn it right off."

"You're not a very good liar, son."

"And that's a good thing, right?"

"I guess so. Try to find something a little more appropriate. There's lots of alternatives."

"Okay, Dad. Right away."

"I'll be home in a couple of hours. And if I see any women's prisons on the TV when I get there, you're going in the Special Housing Unit." Dane knew his son would understand the reference to the SHU from the show.

He ended the call and smiled at Seth, who had begun to shiver. Snow danced in the streetlight behind his head. "You wanna just take one car?" Seth asked. "I can bring you back here once we're done."

"That'd be nice."

Once they got in Seth's car, a Nissan Leaf, Seth turned the heat on and the blower to high. Warmth was coming out in no time. Seth grinned. "Better?"

"Oh God, yes."

"Where to?" Seth asked, putting the car in gear and pulling away from the curb.

"Well, certainly not the Elite. It'll be swamped on fried chicken night."

"It's that good?"

"It's heaven. You'll see. But not tonight." He found himself wanting to take Seth someplace quieter, where they could actually talk and not have to shout to be heard.

"If you make a right up here at Etruria and then go up the hill, you'll be in the part of the town we call the East End. There's a little Italian joint there run by a local family. It's only a bar and a row of booths, but the lasagna's so good it will make you cry. Not to mention gain ten pounds."

"Sounds perfect. And Dane? I don't gain weight. My metabolism still thinks I'm an adolescent boy and burns everything right up. In fact, I'd love to be able to gain ten pounds."

"I hate you," Dane said softly, wondering if he'd be satisfied with the chopped salad they made at D'Angelo's.

"What's that?" Seth asked.

"I said I envy you. I'll have to run five miles in the morning just to stay even."

"You look great. I like a man with a little meat on his bones."

Dane laughed. "Well, I have plenty of that! Meat, I mean." He thought how dirty that sounded, and heat rose to his cheeks. He was glad it was dark in the car. Damn his fair complexion!

Seth didn't say anything, but Dane could see he raised his eyebrows. Whatever that meant….

D'ANGELO'S WAS, as Dane had hoped, quiet. There were a few men at the bar, nursing shot glasses or bottles of beer, watching an old episode of *Mike and Molly* on the TV above the bar. Only one of the four booths was occupied—by an elderly couple whom Dane recognized as the grandparents of one of his honor students last year, who'd gone on to Case Western Reserve University.

He was wondering if he could get away without stopping to talk to them. Harriet, he thought the woman's name was, was a notorious talker. From past experience, Dane knew they'd be stuck for at least fifteen minutes at their table, and he wasn't in the mood.

He wanted to be alone with Seth.

Just then Mary D'Angelo, who owned the place along with her husband, Sam, greeted them. She held a stack of menus and wore a black apron. Her gray hair was cut short.

"Hey, Dane! Just you and your friend tonight, honey?"

"Just us two, Mary. How you been?"

"Good. Good. Can't say the same for Sam, though. He's gotta have that back surgery they've been threatening for years. Goes in the

106

hospital next week." She led them to a booth that just happened to be before they'd pass the older couple's table.

"Thank you, Mary." And Dane really was thankful, in more ways than one. "You tell Sam to take care. I'll keep him in my thoughts and prayers."

"Aw, ain't that sweet?" She waited for them both to sit and handed them menus. "Can I get you guys a beer to start? Maybe a glass of red?"

"Wine would be nice," Seth said. "Chianti?"

"Is there another kind?" Mary asked and laughed. She regarded Seth, then shifted her gaze back to Dane. "Who's your buddy?"

"Mary, this is Seth Wolcott. He just started at the high school this semester. Teaching English and theater."

Mary smiled and nodded. "Well good luck, Seth... and welcome. I'll get you your wine." She hurried away.

Seth looked around the room, and Dane saw it through Seth's eyes. Dane didn't think he'd ever realized how cliché the place was, but also how romantic. The walls were paneled in dark wood, and the lighting was dim, cast by flickering candles in red glass holders on each table and the accent lighting behind the bar. Above them, the ceiling was patterned black tin. The floor was a well-worn checkerboard of black and white. The checkerboard theme continued—quite naturally—with the tablecloths, only these were red and white. The booth seating and bar stools were covered in black vinyl, which had the look and feel of leather. Frank Sinatra was singing over the bar's speaker system, "Strangers in the Night."

"This reminds me of a Billy Joel song," Seth said. "You know the one." He grinned.

Dane filled in, "Scenes from an Italian Restaurant."

Seth nodded, his glee that Dane had picked up so easily on the musical reference apparent. He raised his eyebrows and offered, "Maybe we should get a bottle of red *and* a bottle of white."

Dane chuckled. "You may be able to handle drinking like that on a school night, but I'd be on my ass."

"And wouldn't that be a sight?" Seth looked far away and said softly, "A very pretty sight." He gave Dane an evil grin.

"You're terrible, Mr. Wolcott." Dane felt something akin to helium in his gut—giddy and scared all at once. Was the guy flirting with him? It had been so long since Dane had flirted with anyone of either gender that he really wasn't clear on what signals to look out for. But if Seth was flirting, flattering and exhilarating as it was, Dane was in no way prepared to flirt back. He didn't know how. He wondered if it was even right to flirt with a coworker. And the whole man-on-man thing was hotter than hell, Dane could admit to himself, but also mighty strange to a guy who was so buttoned-up he'd rarely allowed his fantasies to even stray much in that direction over the years of his marriage. So he changed the subject and immediately felt both disappointment and relief at doing what he thought was the right thing.

"So, Seth, how are you adjusting to our little town? Must be a bit of a culture shock, coming from Chicago. I can't imagine."

Seth blew out a sigh. Before he could respond, Mary showed up with their wine and a platter of homemade bread and a little bowl of olive oil and balsamic vinegar infused with crushed red pepper and garlic. She backed away quickly.

"I can't say it's been dull," Seth answered, dipping a piece of bread in the seasoned oil. "It might be small-town, but so far, it's pretty big on excitement. And, sadly, that's not all a good thing." He took a sip of wine.

"Yeah, Truman seems to be the school's punching bag. I think, though, he's beginning to develop some inner strength to deal with those bigots and idiots."

"And that's just what he needs."

"I bet kids were a lot more tolerant in Chicago of people being a little different. I mean, living in such an urban environment must make the kids more sophisticated or something, right?"

Seth snorted. "You'd think! But not really. I mean, yeah, there was more tolerance for gay kids. There was even a gay social and activism club at the school, and it had a pretty good-sized membership, so there were definitely kids who were out. But they still faced the same things Truman does—the bullying and the teasing, the name-calling. Sometimes worse. We had a kid who got bashed right in the school parking lot a couple years ago—poor kid ended up in the hospital with a concussion and a few broken ribs. Not pretty." Seth frowned. "But I guess it is a little easier in a big city, where the kids see gay people all the time."

Dane drank some more of his wine and took his time eating a piece of bread. "What about you?"

"What about me? Was I out? Yeah, sure. The kids all knew. Some of the jock types snickered about it, but really, it was no big deal. And certainly meant nothing to the administration. Hell, our principal was gay."

"I can't imagine." Dane looked away, staring at but not really seeing the specials board mounted above the bar. "I can't believe I came out to the whole school last week." He said it with a feeling akin to shock, as if it were registering just now, as if, really, it was someone else who had taken this step.

Seth smiled, and even in the dim flicker of the candle on their table, Dane could discern the warmth in his eyes. There was something, Dane realized, about the combination of candlelight and a man's eyes that could be mesmerizing. He found it hard to look away.

Seth said, "But don't you feel better now? Now that it's not a secret anymore?"

"I guess." Dane wasn't sure what he felt. He knew if he'd made such an admission at the Catholic school a couple of towns over, he'd probably be seeking new employment.

"Can I tell you something?" Seth asked.

Before Dane could answer, Mary returned. "What did you guys decide on?"

Dane said, "Gosh, Mary, we haven't even looked at the menu."

Most waitresses would have toddled off, saying something to the effect of "take your time," but not Mary. "Hey, don't bother with the menu. Let me tell you what's good tonight. We got a nice big pot of *pasta fagioli*." Mary pronounced it "pasta fazoo." She nodded to Seth, "It's beans and elbow macaroni simmered in a tomato sauce that's to die for. You eat a bowl of that and have some of that bread there, it'll fill you right up." She winked. "And warm you right up too. How does that grab you boys?"

"Sounds delicious," Seth said, and Dane nodded.

"Two bowls, then? I'll bring you a nice escarole salad to start." She walked away.

"I like her," Seth said.

"I do too. She's sweet and salty. Like the mother you always wished you had," Dane said. "But you said you wanted to tell me something."

"I did?" Seth asked.

Dane had the feeling Seth's innocent act was just that—an act. "Yeah."

"Slipped my mind." He looked around. "Hope she brings those salads right out. I'm starving."

Dane wondered if Seth realized his foot rested on Dane's instep. He was pretty sure he did. Seth didn't strike him as the unobservant type. Dane shifted in the booth, wishing he could readjust the erection growing downward in his pants.

It was both painful and pleasurable.

CHAPTER 13

DANE FELL asleep later that night thinking about Seth, who had never followed up on the answer to the question, "Can I tell you something?"

What had he been going to say? Dane wondered. Here, in the privacy of his own bed, he wanted to believe Seth was about to utter flattering words, or something along the lines of wanting to see Dane again. But such thoughts were quickly quashed by the realization Dane was lying there in the bed he'd once shared with his wife. On sheets she'd picked out at the local Walmart, under a quilt she had made one winter when she was inspired by the idea of taking up the craft. Dane tossed in the bed, made uncomfortable by the polar opposite ends of his thoughts.

And the guilt. He was a widower, for Christ's sake. And Seth was a peer, a coworker. What was the crude way his dad, a welder, had once put it? "You don't shit where you eat." Yeah. Lovely. But it was true. He'd seen enough teacher-teacher romances go south to know the common-sense thing to do was to avoid them. The result was never pretty when they didn't work out.

Whatever awaited Dane out there in terms of meeting—and connecting with—a man, it probably shouldn't be with someone with whom he worked. The fact that Seth was so in his radar, and *so* cute and *so* gay, was convenient, but it probably wasn't a good idea.

He turned over again and punched his pillow into submission. Was it just proximity that attracted him to Seth? Or was there something else? Maybe something about how their gazes connected and held in delicious suspension until one or the other forced himself to look away. Or maybe it was that Seth seemed genuinely interested in him. That fact, and Dane didn't think he was exaggerating, was as terrifying as it was exhilarating. He could imagine the two of them together in all sorts of settings, and not just the naughty ones—although there were plenty of those when he allowed his mind, and his id, to wander—but also simple domestic scenes. He could see cooking his mother's pot roast for Seth, or snuggling up in a darkened room with a shared bowl of popcorn between them as they watched a movie together, covered by his grandma's windowpane-patterned afghan. There was this incredible mix of sweet and sexy both within Seth and within Dane's own fantasies.

No. I can't entertain thoughts of seeing another teacher. That's just wrong. For Christ's sake, think of Clarissa. She goes to the school. Can you imagine how hard it would be for her to deal? I mean, she hasn't come anywhere near to terms with accepting my gayness, let alone the idea that I might be hooking up with another faculty member. The thought made Dane laugh, but it was a giddy sort of laugh, born of a kind of excited hysteria.

The words "hooking up with another teacher" put a match to the flame of Dane's desire, entirely unexpectedly. And completely unbidden, an image rose up in his head of Seth spread out, not on a bed, but on his desk at school. In this almost involuntary fantasy, Seth was naked and prone on his back on the desk, his legs in the air.

Dane felt his breath coming a little quicker as he mentally eyed up Seth's taut body, the fine dusting of hair he imagined on his chest and then narrowing down in a thin line across his navel—an innie— and then to another burst of hair that provided a frame for a gorgeous uncut cock rising up, its purple head oozing precome and just peeking out of its sheath.

Dane couldn't help it. He touched himself and, with very little effort, squirted into his boxer briefs.

The image of Seth on the desk vanished, as though it were a wisp of smoke and a strong wind had come along. Dane shook his head, troubled that he had let his mind *go there*, but suddenly so tired. It was as though his orgasm, powerful as it was, had drained the life from him.

He knew he should get up and go in the bathroom and clean himself off. He knew he should put on clean underwear, but all the energy he could muster was only enough to struggle out of the boxers, wipe himself with them, and fling them on the floor beside the bed.

Sleep came to him quickly, like deliverance.

THIS TIME they're in a room that seems vaguely familiar to Dane. Maybe it's someplace they'd once stayed on a vacation, perhaps in the Appalachians. The room has the look of a cabin, with its knotty pine walls and early American furniture. Again, there's silence as Dane moves through the room.

Katy is seated in front of a fieldstone fireplace. Flames dance and flicker before her, and she wears an emerald green sweater, one Dane remembers because it looks so good with her auburn hair.

She doesn't seem aware that he's there.

He creeps softly up to her, wondering if this time he'll see her face. It's weird he has this consciousness, he thinks, even within the confines of the dream.

He stands directly behind her. There is no sound. The only light is from the flickering golden and orange illumination of the blaze in the fireplace.

He's afraid to look at her, afraid that when he tries to see her face, he will only get the back of her head again—which is an image ripped straight out of a nightmare.

And he doesn't want this to be a nightmare.

So he leans forward slowly, gently, as though he doesn't want her to realize he's there, so close. He whispers, "Katy?"

She turns to him. His heart gives a little leap because he can see her face, her smile.

She stares at him, and even in the dull, flickering light, her green eyes are alive. She's alive. His Katy.

She reaches up with her hand to touch him, and he reaches out with his own, but it seems their fingertips just can't connect.

Not for a real touch.

They are this far apart, an inch, maybe less.

Her voice breaks the silence. "I'm okay, Dane."

Dane finds his own voice isn't accessible. He moves his lips, yet nothing emerges.

Katy says, "And so are you."

Dane sat up suddenly in bed. His room was filled with the slate gray light peculiar to dawn. He looked to his side, expecting Katy to be there, perhaps snoring softly.

It took a moment for his conscious mind to catch up. He let out a small laugh and felt grateful for having had this moment with Katy. He lay back down and wondered, *Did she know? Had she always known?*

Across town, in his little one-bedroom apartment, Seth lay in his own bed. Like Dane, he too had fallen asleep wondering what he would have said if Dane had answered his question, "Can I tell you something?"

Seth had drifted off thinking the *something* revolved around his attraction to Dane, from the very first moment he had laid eyes on him in the school parking lot. He would have said that the mere sight of Dane had taken his breath away. And it wasn't just physical—although there was plenty of that. It was also kind of spiritual, if that was the right word. Seth had seen thousands of handsome men, and they always registered with a silent little "woof" in his brain, but there was something more when he saw Dane, something soulful, an innate knowledge that this was a good man.

He would have gone on to tell Dane that he didn't know where these feelings—so strong he couldn't deny them—had come from. He didn't *want* to find someone new. Lord no! Not after having his heart stomped on and his faith shaken in relationships so resoundingly back in Chicago.

He had come to Summitville to get away, to be single for a long time, to just teach and appreciate the treasures solitude could bring.

His last thought before slumber took over was, *Damn you, Dane! Toppling all my carefully laid plans.*

And now, lying awake as dawn crept in around his blinds, he recalled snatches of dream, images that might have been what brought him to sudden and jarring consciousness.

114

He had been following Dane on a beach. Maybe it was a Lake Michigan beach in Chicago. There was the requisite tall grass and aquamarine waters, looking tropical the way even the lake could on hot summer days. Dane wore only a pair of board shorts, imprinted with a pattern of sea turtles on an orange background as he strode away from Seth. Or maybe he was leading Seth somewhere? Whatever the case, Seth remembered that he liked the view from back there: Dane's broad shoulders, kissed with freckles from the sun; his smooth back, tapering down into his shorts; his calves, crowned with golden hair, so shapely and muscular.

Suddenly Dane vanished from sight, and even in the dream, Seth believed he knew he was dreaming and this was just a trick of that odd state.

But it wasn't.

As Seth moved forward, he saw there was a huge chasm in the sand, as though the earth itself had ripped open, cracked.

Down in the abyss, Dane crouched, looking up at him, terror in his eyes.

Seth couldn't remember if Dane had said anything.

The last image he had was of getting down on his belly so he could reach down to Dane. He stretched his arm, his hand out to Dane.

Had their fingers met?

Seth turned over. He wished he knew.

The wind rattled his windows. The room brightened, and his furniture, all of it rental, all of it vaguely Scandinavian, became more defined.

It was time to face another day.

CHAPTER 14

TRUMAN LEANED against the sink in the bathroom, examining his face closely. Both Mr. Wolcott and Mr. Bernard told him essentially the same thing: be true to yourself.

Don't hide it.

Don't be ashamed of it.

Who was he, anyway?

He was *exactly* what all the bullies tormented him about. He was a big sissy. There was no denying it. He had realized, through the long, sleepless night before his return to school today, that he had two choices when it came to being that sissy.

One: He could butch it up and pretend to be someone else. Just like he found glorious retro finds at the Goodwill, he knew he could also find a Carhartt jacket, work boots, jeans, and flannel shirts in a multitude of hues. Or he could go for the jock look—sneaks, sweatpants, and a sports logo'd T-shirt or sweatshirt. He could give himself a buzz cut and leave his curly blond locks on the bathroom floor. He could work to change his walk to a John Wayne swagger. He could pitch his voice lower. He could withdraw so deep down inside himself that no one would recognize him.

And that damn sissy, the one who had caused him so much trouble, would be banished, never to be seen again. Not even in the mirror.

Or....

Two: He could embrace who he was. Celebrate his inner and outer sissy. As Patsy had told him, time and time again, he was just as the Lord had made him. "The Lord," Patsy always said, "doesn't make mistakes, honey. It's that simple. If there were anything wrong with who or what you are, you wouldn't have been born that way. And believe me, you *were* born that way. I saw it with my own eyes."

Being a sissy didn't have to mean he was weak. It didn't have to mean he was like a girl—and even if he was like a girl, so what? Why was that something bad? Why was that something to be ridiculed? Girls could be strong and smart—so what if he emulated them? His own mother was one, and look at her. She didn't have much, but she took care of him and loved him fiercely... with an adoration and protectiveness that verged on ferocious.

He was a sissy. The choice—which was never a choice at all—was clear. He had to be who he was, to play the cards he'd been dealt. If he didn't, well, he'd just be cheating.

And even if there was a way he *could* change, the one person he'd never be able to hide his true self from was himself. And what a horror that would be, to go through life masquerading as someone else.

No. Whether he was good or whether he was bad was immaterial. He was Truman.

He stepped back away from the sink to admire himself in the mirror, and he gasped and then laughed—just a little. The person looking back at him was still him, but a stronger, more concentrated version.

A more beautiful version. His soul shone through.

Today might be a horrible day. But it was going to be on his own terms.

He turned for himself in the mirror once more. It was a good thing Patsy had worked herself to exhaustion the night before, because Truman had used the bathroom for two hours to get himself ready for school.

He paused before opening the bathroom door and heading out. He paused to blow himself a kiss in the mirror.

PATSY AWAKENED to the smell of coffee and bacon. Was there anything better to wake up to? Well, maybe next to that professional wrestler, John Cena. But barring that, coffee and bacon were pretty close to heaven.

She rolled over in bed and looked at the alarm clock. It was just past seven, so Truman was not only fixing breakfast, bless his heart, he was up, which meant he wasn't going to try to avoid going back to school, something she'd worried about and dreaded. She had imagined having to physically tug him by his hands into the car and then forcibly propel him into the school, her hands firmly on his back.

She didn't want to be cast in that role.

She sat up, rubbing the small of her back. It ached from being on her feet all last evening. Her quilted housecoat hung on a hook behind the bedroom door, and she shrugged into it, the aromas wafting in from the kitchen making her mouth water and her fatigue begin to clear.

She pulled back the curtains and looked outside. It was one of those winter days, Patsy knew, that was deceptive. It was bright outside, the sun rising brilliantly, gloriously, and the sky a crystalline blue, seamless and forever. The snow on the ground reflected it all back, nearly blinding. And when the wind kicked up some of the white stuff, it looked like diamonds in the air.

Pretty, Patsy thought, *and probably close to lethal.* As though timed, her alarm clock sprung to life, and the announcer's voice out of nearby Pittsburgh told her that it was currently twelve below in most parts of the tri-state area that morning and temperatures were not expected to rise above zero.

If Herman would start, and that was always a big if with that piece of shit, she would have to drive Truman to school this morning. She didn't want her baby out for longer than necessary in this cold, even if it was only to wait for the bus.

She headed for the bathroom and, on the way, shouted to Truman, "Good morning, sweetie! Thanks for getting breakfast going. You're a peach!"

"How do you want your eggs, Mom?"

"Scrambled. Like my brains." She went into the bathroom and sat on the toilet. After she finished, she looked at the countertop around the sink. It looked like a beauty school explosion had taken place. Almost all her makeup had been taken down from the medicine cabinet. There was a crumpled box of Special Effects hair dye in the wastebasket in a shade called "Cupcake Pink." Patsy had no idea where *that* had come from.

She washed her hands and tried to ignore the nagging feeling developing in the pit of her gut. "Lord, what's he gone and done?" she wondered aloud to her reflection.

There was only one way to find out. She slipped from the bathroom and stepped into the kitchen. It wasn't a long journey in a house that totaled only about 800 square feet.

And there her boy was, at the stove, turning bacon. He turned to smile at her.

Patsy smiled back. Her breath caught in her throat, and without thinking about it, she clutched the front of her housecoat. She wanted to freeze this moment in time, file it prominently in her mental book of family images.

Her boy was beautiful. Radiant.

A truer, better version of himself.

SETH WAS glad he was the first to lay eyes on Truman as he emerged from the beat-up Dodge Neon that morning. He'd wanted the chance to accompany the kid to homeroom, just to make sure everything was okay. He wanted Truman's first day back to go smoothly, with no undue stress.

Truman waved to his mother, whom Seth could see behind the wheel. The car sputtered smoke out of its exhaust and sounded more like a diesel truck than a compact car. Truman turned to him, so bundled up that Seth wouldn't have placed him if he hadn't first seen Patsy at the wheel. He reminded Seth of Kenny from *South Park*.

Truman's down coat had its collar pulled up, shielding his lower face. The top half was also nearly hidden under a bright red woolen cap, pulled down so low that all one could see were Truman's eyes.

Seth smiled and started toward the boy. "Hey there! Good morning. Glad I ran into you."

"Hcy, Mr. Wolcott." Truman lagged a little behind as Seth led the way to the double doors, which were open for the brief period between first bell and final, tardy bell.

Other kids swarmed around them.

Once they were inside, Seth walked with Truman to his locker. He repeated what he'd told him before, how he and "Mr. Bernard" would both be there for him, especially today, when Truman was trying to make what had to be a difficult reentry back into the high school. "Anytime," he told Truman, "Even if I'm in class. You come get me if there's anything you need."

"Sure, Mr. Wolcott," Truman said.

The tone and tenor of Truman's voice was good, strong and not indicative of nervousness or fear. Seth felt a bit of relief creep in. Maybe things would be okay. At least for today.

Truman removed his hat, so the first thing Seth noticed was his hair.

A bright pink stripe now divided his pale blond hair down the middle. Seth didn't mean to, but he gave out a little gasp. He chuckled.

Truman turned to him to ask, "You like it?" He pulled off his coat and turned back around to hang it in his locker.

And that's when Seth saw the rest—the eyeliner, the lip gloss, the oh-so-subtle touch of blusher on Truman's pale cheeks.

Truman repeated, "Do you like it?" He grinned. "You said I should be myself. I think that's some solid advice." He removed his coat to reveal the white T-shirt emblazoned with its homemade design and legend across the chest in jagged letters:

Sissies Rule.

He had paired the T with his dowdiest accompaniment—relatively speaking, anyway—a pair of skinny black jeans. On his feet, sensibly distressed combat boots.

He looked like a cross between RuPaul and Billy Idol.

"I will accept any of the 'f' words in regard to my appearance," Truman said, smiling. "Fierce. Fabulous. Fine. Even ferocious." He shook his head and wagged a finger at Seth. "But not faggy. Unless, of course, I say it. If I say it, I own it."

Seth could feel kids in the hallway stopping behind them. Stopping to stare. Stopping to giggle. Seth had an urge, and hated himself for it, to shield the boy from their view.

120

But what was he supposed to do with this? Sure, he'd told Truman to hold his head up high, to be proud of who he was, to love himself. But he didn't know Truman would take things to this extreme.

In his own odd way, Truman looked adorable, Seth thought. It was what an old friend of his back in Chicago referred to as "genderfuck," or playing around with conventions of male and female and challenging them, reclaiming them, and most importantly, defining for yourself alone how *you* would interpret them.

Along with the sound of snickering, there were whispers. And Seth thought, *Here we go again.* Without thinking, he took hold of Truman's arm and led him toward the office. He knew the school's guidance counselor office sat empty. The position had fallen victim to budget cuts, necessitated by a levy that had failed during the last election.

"Tru-woman! *Lovely* to see you!" A kid in a varsity letterman jacket called out, and his posse guffawed.

"Did you see that fag?" one guy wondered to his buddy as they passed.

Once inside the office, Seth closed the door. "Truman. Are you sure you wanna do this?" Seth himself wasn't certain how he should proceed. On the one hand, he didn't want to see Truman set himself up for more ridicule and pain. But on the other, in a weird, stronger way, he was proud of the kid and, yes, his courage. Truman had taken Seth's message of self-love and strength to an extreme, sure, but it demonstrated strength of character and an unwillingness to accept anything less than life on his own terms. Seth didn't want to be the one to wipe out that new and, he suspected, very fragile sense of self.

And Truman came back to him with what Seth thought was the best answer possible.

"Look. Kids here hate me. Right? They think I'm weird. They think I'm a queer, a sissy, a fag, a *pantywaist*. You name it, I've been called it. Nobody wants to be around me. I guess they think they'll be tainted somehow by gay cooties." He giggled. "So why bother?"

"What do you mean?" Seth asked, although in the back of his mind, he knew he already had the answer.

Truman shrugged. "Why not just be who I am? They're gonna hate me either way, so why not have some fun with it? Show them I don't give a crap about their opinion of me. Because I *am* what they say." He looked at Seth. "I *own* it." He pointed to the legend on his shirt: "Sissies Rule."

Seth plopped down in the guest chair in the small office and shook his head but was unable to keep the smile from his face. "They do indeed," he said softly. He then looked up at Truman. "But what if no one agrees with you?"

Truman smirked. "They never did to begin with. This isn't about other people. This is about me. I don't want to spend my whole life being someone else, what someone else thinks I should be. I want to be me. I don't want to look in the mirror and see a person I don't recognize."

"Wow. I couldn't have said that better myself. Truman, I have to warn you, though, you're going to—"

Truman held up a hand, cutting him off. "I think I know what you're going to say. I'm in for a world of hurt. People, especially kids my age, can be cruel." He shrugged. "I realized I don't care. I'd rather be different than one of the crowd."

"That's some very good thinking." Seth stood up as the final bell for homeroom sounded. "We both need to get going. Stay fierce. Stay strong. And know that I am here for you."

They started from the room. Seth reached out to lay a hand on Truman's shoulder. He felt so bony, so insubstantial that a wave of protectiveness rose up in Seth's gut. "I have a prediction for you."

Truman glanced over his shoulder.

"You're going to find people like you. Compatriots. Others who march to the beat of a different drummer. Maybe not today. Maybe not next year. And maybe it will only be a scattered few, but I promise you, they're out there. And when you find one another, you'll know. And they will be family."

Truman stopped for a moment. He peered into Seth's eyes. "Thanks, Mr. Wolcott. I'll keep my eyes peeled." He grinned and hurried away.

"God help him," Seth whispered to himself and headed off to homeroom.

IT WAS Dane's free period. Normally during this hour he'd hang out in the teacher's lounge, ostensibly to grade papers and catch up on his lesson planning, but the truth was it was a time to gossip and joke around with his fellow teachers, a release valve, a break in the daily adolescent battles with people who understood.

But ever since he'd made his admission to practically the entire school that he was gay, Dane felt better being off by himself. Not that anyone treated him any differently. There was a surprising lack of interest among his fellow teachers, and in fact Betsy Wagner had suddenly seemed to take *more* of an interest in him than she ever had, as though he'd become someone different from who she encountered every day since she'd begun working at the school five years ago. Dane almost felt like a victim of reverse discrimination.

So he spent his free period alone in his classroom with the door closed and the lights off. It wasn't exactly sitting in the dark, since one wall was all windows above the storage shelves. There was a lot of light streaming in. He sat on one of these shelves now, staring out at the valley spread below him, watching the Ohio River's curve as it made its way south toward a rendezvous with the Mississippi.

The class just before his free period, freshman composition, had been... how should he put it? Different? Interesting? Terrifying? It seemed there were no words in the English language, or at least in Dane's vocabulary, that could describe the complicated feelings that arose within the confines of that fifty-five minute period.

Maybe it would have gone a different way if Truman hadn't been the last one to enter the class.

Just before he came into the room, the class was, as always, abuzz—lots of laughter, whispers, hurried conversations before the second bell rang and everyone simmered down. Or at least that's what they were supposed to do. Dane usually had to yell or say something shocking to put an end to the classroom chatter.

Not today.

Today, Truman made his entrance.

The class went immediately silent. It was like some divine hand reached out and with a tap, hit the Mute button. The class went so silent so fast it was almost eerie. Mouths dropped open. Eyes actually widened.

And it wasn't just his students who reacted with stunned silence. Dane was frozen too. There was Truman, the kid who usually tried to hide behind the pile of books and notebooks he always carried under one arm, eyes cast downward. But today there was Truman, the unwitting—or was he?—center of attention.

Pink hair. Makeup. And the T-shirt with its legend about sissies.

Dane was taken aback. Should he pull Truman from the class? Take him into the hallway and try to explain that he had taken things too far? That he was only courting his own downfall? That the best he could hope for by day's end was name-calling and the worst, a beating or two?

There wasn't time for that. It would have only drawn more attention to the boy, and that was the last thing Truman needed, as far as Dane saw it.

He watched as Truman made his way to his assigned seat near the back of the classroom. On his way there, a pudgy kid named Adam Lance, with a face like a French bulldog's, stuck out his foot to trip Truman.

Truman stopped, put his hands on his hips, and stared down at the offending foot. He cocked his head. The silence seemed to expand, and Dane watched as Adam's face began to color.

Truman pointed to the foot. "You might want to put that back under the desk where it belongs. A person could trip and break something." Truman made a little gesture, a flick of his wrist, indicating that Adam's foot belonged under his desk and not in the aisle.

Truman did not move, and Adam sat there stymied, Dane thought, but also not moving.

Finally, Truman said, "You missed out, Lance. You didn't get to trip me. Not today. Better luck tomorrow."

Truman continued to stand there until finally, with a sheepish grin and a roll of his eyes, Adam Lance put his foot back under his desk.

Truman smirked, said "Thank you," and took his seat.

Dane's lesson plan was all but forgotten. His mind felt like someone had come in with a Swiffer and dusted away any preparation he had made. He drummed his fingers on his desk and finally stood.

He licked his lips and addressed his class. Today needed to be something beyond the vagaries of dangling participles. Without really planning what he was going to say, he simply asked, "So, what does everyone think?"

No one responded until Dane prompted the class again. They simply stared at him with bovine eyes, as if he too had dyed his hair pink. It was like he'd asked the question in Mandarin Chinese.

He cleared his throat and glanced back quickly at Truman to gauge his reaction. Truman simply met his gaze with interest. Dane looked away and repeated, "So. What does everyone think of Truman's new look?"

Adam Lance was, predictably, the first to pipe up. "He looks like a fag. Course he always looks like a fag, but today he ramped it up. Called in the big guns." He snickered.

There were a few nervous titters before the class returned to silence. A few people shifted in their seats. Dane thought this wasn't what they were expecting, and maybe it made some of them uncomfortable.

"What does a 'fag' look like, Adam?" Dane wanted to know. "Although I should stop here and correct you. Maybe you should refer to gay people as just that: gay. Or lesbian." Dane smiled. "Or LGBT." He stepped forward, a little closer to the class. "Or maybe just human, but perhaps that's too broad for you. Maybe that scares you because it would necessarily include you under the same umbrella." He drew in a breath and moved forward to stand directly above. "So tell us, so we know, what a gay person looks like. To you."

Adam looked desperately around the room, his narrow piggy eyes hungry for someone to take his side. But Dane noted that no one would even return his gaze.

"I don't know," he finally said.

He opened a spiral-bound notebook and began furiously staring at it, his face crimson. The notebook page, Dane noticed, was blank.

Dane moved away. "I'm sorry, Adam. You seemed so sure, I just thought you could enlighten us." He let his gaze roam over the rest of the class, all with expressions Dane could read as "Please don't call on me. Just please—don't." He had to ask, though. He'd dived into the pool headfirst, in a manner of speaking, and the only way not to drown was to swim. "So, anyone else? Does someone else have the courage to say what they think of Truman's look today?"

Bonnie Petrovich, a girl with curly dark hair and big eyes who was president of the John 3:16 Club at the school, raised her hand timidly.

"Bonnie?"

"It's wrong," she said. "Boys aren't supposed to look like him. It's unnatural."

Dane nodded. He didn't want to jump all over the girl and make her defensive. He wanted this to be an open and honest dialogue. So he held in check a lot of things he wanted to say and instead asked, "Unnatural? What makes it that way?"

She squirmed and slid down lower in her seat. "I guess it's the makeup. Boys aren't supposed to wear makeup."

"And it says that in what? The Bible?"

Bonnie tittered—a nervous laugh. "No. I don't think so, anyway." She rolled her eyes and sat up a little straighter. "I'll check and get back to you on that."

"Then what makes it unnatural, Bonnie? I notice you have a little makeup on yourself today. Is that blue eye shadow I see?"

The class laughed. And Bonnie slumped lower in her seat. Softly, she replied, "But I'm a girl."

"Yes, you are. And a very pretty one," Dane said. "And I would imagine you're a girl who gets up in the morning and decides what she'll wear, even what makeup she might apply. Why do you do that?"

"Because I want to look decent, respectable when I'm at school."

"Okay. But why do you make the choices you do? Why not green eye shadow? Or high heels over those... what are those?"

"Hunter boots," Bonnie filled in.

"Got it. So you make choices in the morning. Why?"

"I'm not sure what you mean."

"Let me try to help. I would say that all of us, to a degree, when we dress ourselves, or style our hair, or—for some of us—put on a little blush and lip gloss, we're making choices in how we want the world to perceive us. Clothes, hair, makeup, all of these things are visual cues to the world about who we are. Don't you agree, Bonnie?"

"I guess so."

"Maybe Truman doesn't want to hide." Dane looked back at Truman, whose attention was now rapt, laser-focused on Dane's face. "Truman, do you have anything to say? Maybe you can help us understand the decisions *you* made this morning."

Truman shook his head. "No, sir."

Dane didn't want to put the boy on the spot any more than he already had. He was about to ask the class again about self-expression and how we want the world to perceive us when Truman piped up in a trembling yet strong voice. "My appearance speaks for itself."

Dane nodded. He went back to his desk, where he reclined on the edge of it, gnawing for a moment on a pencil he picked up from its surface. He thought about how he himself was dressed today: a pair of Dockers khakis, a button-down blue Oxford-cloth shirt with the sleeves rolled up, a pair of clean running shoes. The outfit was pretty much his uniform. He looked like the male version of a soccer mom, he thought.

But was it him?

Do we dress the way we do to show the world who we are or to hide it?

While he thought these things, Alicia Adams, a black girl who lived in the same neighborhood as Truman and had a fondness for hoodies and running pants, tentatively raised her hand, looking around with fearful brown eyes. Dane couldn't remember if the girl had ever spoken up in class before.

"I think it's kind of cool, you know," Alicia began. "Truman's, like, brave to dress like that."

"Brave?" Dane asked, echoing what he thought might be the question on the majority's mind. Brave seemed an odd conclusion to draw from pink hair and mascara… on a boy.

"Yeah. It don't take no courage to throw on a pair of jeans, some sneaks, and a T-shirt. Anybody can do that."

"Doesn't take any," Dane said.

"Yeah, yeah, whatever. What I'm sayin', though, is that Truman, by dressin' like that, is being fierce, fearless. You say how we dress is a way of saying who we are. And I think Truman is doin' just that—and it might get his face punched in. Or"—she looked over at Adam Lance—"tripped by some joke-ass motherfucker who thinks he cool." She looked at Dane. "Sorry, Mr. Bernard."

"It's okay. Just watch it."

"But I think Truman has more goin' on than most of these kids at this school who just follow the crowd. He's bein' true to who he is."

She smiled, and it transformed her face, infusing it with warmth and compassion. Dane couldn't help but smile back.

"And I like that." She swiveled toward Truman and gave him a smile.

"I like it too," Dane surprised himself by saying.

He glanced back at Truman, who grinned, then gazed down at his desk as though embarrassed.

"Anyone else?" Dane asked, but no one else spoke up. Truman—shy, meek little Truman—had silenced them all. Dane hoped Truman felt a little inkling of power in that.

And now, back in the present, back in his free period, Dane wondered how the rest of Truman's day had gone, was going. Had he survived? Triumphed? Had the world beaten him—and his optimism—back into submission?

He let his head loll back, thinking it could only be one of two ways with no room for in-betweens. It was either disaster or triumph.

CHAPTER 15

DANE WATCHED Clarissa study her iPhone. He took in the small, wiry frame, the auburn hair, one lock of which she twisted relentlessly, so much so that Dane feared she would pull it out by its roots. *She looks so much like her mother; it breaks my heart. It also breaks my heart that she can suddenly find little more than a word or two to say to me. We used to talk to each other.*

He was just about to ask her if she wanted him to order a pizza for dinner when his own iPhone spoke up. He glanced down at its screen—Seth. They were due that evening to stop over at Truman's once more for their weekly talk. He figured this week they'd have a ton to discuss, since Truman's appearance at the school over the past several days had always been unusual, to say the least, and colorful, to try to put it in a good light. And it *was* a good light. Truman had come bursting out of his closet with rainbow-colored flames. And if you didn't like it? You could go to hell.

"Hey, Seth," he said softly, for some reason not wanting to disturb his daughter. He backed from the entryway to the family room into the kitchen. "What's up?"

"I just got off the phone with Patsy. She called for Truman and said, with more than a little pride, that her boy doesn't think it's necessary for us to come by anymore."

"What? You think that's wise?"

Seth didn't say anything for a moment or two. "You're asking the wrong person about wisdom. I'm beginning to think maybe Truman has more of that stuff in his possession than even I do. I'm proud of that kid. And I can't really say that his not wanting to see us is such a bad thing, especially if the kid is feeling confident, much more than we expected. I think it's okay to just let him be. See where things go. I have a feeling that if Truman needs us, he'll let us know."

Dane didn't know if leaving Truman alone was such a good idea. The boy was almost acting out. He was on the manic side of the manic-depressive scale. It was obvious he didn't have much money for fashion, but he had a surplus of imagination, and each day he was able to craft another startling statement ensemble from things he'd gotten at the local thrift stores and rummage sales, Dane suspected. Yesterday he wore a pair of fuchsia-and-lime-green-striped stretch pants with a lime green hoodie and the ever-present combat boots. Dane suspected the pants he'd swiped from Patsy. They were nearly the same size.

Truman was still getting teased and laughed at, that was for sure, but Dane was surprised to realize, when he thought about it, that it wasn't as much or as frequently. But it still seemed to him that Truman was taunting fate, and he told Seth so. "He's headed for trouble, wearing those clothes...."

"I don't know about that," Seth said. "Yeah, the things he's been wearing to school do make him a target." He snickered. "They often border on the ridiculous, but sometimes, sometimes...." His voice trailed off.

"Yeah?"

"Sometimes he looks pretty cool. And cute. Whatever it is, I've noticed this week, people are backing off. He's still facing being ostracized, but I don't see the bullying anymore. I don't see people laughing as much. It's as if he's taken control of the ridicule, owning it like he says, and I think some of the kids are starting to respect that. He's even made a friend, I think, and *that's* something I didn't know if I'd ever see."

"Alicia Adams?" Dane had seen the girl who'd defended him in her class having lunch with Truman only yesterday. The girl had always taken a backseat to her tall and gifted-for-basketball older brother, Darrell. She stood out more now with Truman by her side, the two of them walking down the hall together, laughing, heads close like conspirators.

"Yeah. Yeah. So maybe, I don't know, maybe if Truman takes charge and shows he isn't afraid of being weird, of presenting himself in a way that makes sense to him, some of the kids are starting to respect that. You know, it's like if he calls himself queer first and wears the clothes to prove it, he takes the wind out of the sails of those who want to tease or bully him about it."

"I get it," Dane said quietly, not sure that he did. Dane had spent his whole life hiding, and while he couldn't say it made for pure happiness, it did make for him fitting in. He leaned around the edge of the kitchen archway to peer into the family room. He wouldn't have those kids in there if he'd been "himself."

"Listen," Seth said. "Just because we're not seeing Truman doesn't mean you and I can't get together, does it?"

Dane smiled and felt a flush of warmth course through him. He was surprised Seth was asking. He'd figured he was just calling to tell him the "counseling" was off for that night. "I don't see why not. I need to order a pizza for the kids. And then maybe we could meet up somewhere?"

Seth said, "How about if you just come by my place? I have an apartment downtown, if you could call my neighborhood a downtown. I mean, it's, like, four streets." Seth chuckled.

Dane laughed. "And don't forget the Diamond," Dane said, calling out the fountained intersection where those four streets met.

"How could I? I look down on the fountain from my window. Did they ever actually have water in that thing?"

"They will. In the summer. And colored lights. And before you got here in January, that's where they put the city Christmas tree. We all stand around it and hold hands and sing that song from *How the Grinch Stole Christmas*."

"Sure you do," Seth laughed. "I picked the right place, then. Pizza sounds good. I could order too. That is, if you want to come over?" Dane thought he heard a little wariness edge into Seth's voice.

Dane wasn't sure. Well, he *was* sure. An evening with Seth alone was something that caused his heart to thump in his chest. *But what will happen? Shouldn't I stay home with my kids?*

You're home with your kids almost every night. They ignore you for the most part. Go. It'll be fine. You'll be fine.

"It's only pizza," Seth said.

"What?" Dane gasped and felt like his mind was being read. "I didn't say it was anything else." Before he gave himself wiggle room to back out, he said, "I like sausage and mushrooms on mine, if that's okay."

"That's more than okay," Seth said. "It's perfect. Give me an hour, okay? I need to phone in the order and take a shower."

Dane wanted to ask what he needed to take a shower for, then laughed internally at himself for his panic. *People often take showers after a long day at work. It doesn't mean he's cleaning up—or out—for you.* At the thought, Dane felt fire rise to his cheeks. Before he said something totally stupid, he said, "See you in an hour, then," and hung up quickly.

SETH CLICKED off the call. He moved into the kitchen, where he'd already established a "junk" drawer in one of the cabinets. He'd filled it with pens, pencils, a guide to his cable TV, instructions for his Mr. Coffee, and what he was looking for—the magazine-thin tri-state phone book. He opened it to the yellow pages to find a couple of different pizza places that delivered and wished he had asked Dane for a recommendation.

He chose the one that was truly local—the other was a Papa John's—called them and placed an order for a large sausage and mushroom. They didn't ask if he wanted deep dish, stuffed, or thin crust, and Seth remembered, once again, he was no longer in Chicago. He gave his address, and they promised to arrive within the half hour. "That's fast," he sputtered, but his order taker had already hung up.

He hurried around the one-bedroom, straightening, swiping his hand across his dusty coffee table, and rinsing and stacking dishes in the sink—the apartment, which looked like it had last been decorated during the Carter administration, did not have a dishwasher. He stripped the bed and put on clean sheets. "You never know!" He laughed at himself. He then stripped down and stepped into the shower.

As he stood under the spray from the showerhead, he told himself this was not a date, as much as he might like it to be. This man he now had to acknowledge he had fallen for was most likely not even ready for a date, especially not with another man. Another man who was his coworker. A romance between the two of them was wrong for all sorts of reasons.

It was a bad idea on so many levels, Seth didn't even want to try and count. He soaped his ass crack. He soaped his dick and balls and, leaving them lathered, took his razor to them, rinsing and repeating until they were as smooth and hairless as a baby's bottom. "Not that anyone will be touching them," he reminded the tile shower enclosure.

After toweling off, he threw open his closet and dresser drawers to try to decide what to wear. "What's it matter?" he asked himself. "You're just having a colleague over for dinner. Nothing more."

Seth pulled out his favorite pair of Levi's, which were worn and soft, faded to the palest of blues, with the knees pretty much worn away. He knew without looking how they gripped his ass, how the worn denim accentuated and highlighted his crotch. Buttoning them, he repeated, "Yup. Just having a colleague over for dinner. Wait a minute, didn't I forget underwear? Ah well, it's too late now." He looked down to see the outline of his cock head in the denim. "Naughty," he whispered and watched as the head inched upward a bit, as though he'd called it by name.

And maybe he had.

He paired the jeans with a navy blue V-neck cashmere sweater that showed off his pec muscles and broad shoulders to very good advantage, if he said so himself. And he did.

He looked through the shoes lined up under his bed and, in the end, decided on bare feet.

"It's just a casual night in with a fellow teacher. We'll discuss what our favorite novels are to teach, which ones really get the kids involved."

Seth jumped when he heard the buzz of the intercom from downstairs. He looked out the window, in spite of the fact that the building's call box was in an alcove. All he saw was the darkened streets and fountain below, the blinking yellow traffic light crying out that this was a town where nothing ever happened—not even a car crash. He'd learned quickly that the talk-and-listen feature of the little box next to his front door no longer worked, so he simply buzzed in whoever was down there, thinking it could only be one of two people: the delivery person or Dane.

It seemed too early for either.

He listened at the door for the trudge of footsteps on the stairs and then in his rose-patterned carpeted hallway. When those footfalls reached his front door, he swung the door open with a big grin. Man or pizza—both were good reasons to smile.

But the smile flickered out quickly when Seth saw who was standing there.

"What the fuck?" Seth asked.

DANE PARKED his car around the corner from Seth's building. Although it was called the Little Building, it was, at four stories, the tallest building in Summitville's dying downtown.

The night was not as bitter cold as it had been, even though it was clear. The black sky above him was sprinkled with stars. A crescent moon shone its silvery glow down on him as he hurried to Seth's front entrance. He clutched a tall brown paper sack in his hand. In it was a bottle of Chianti. He thought it might remind Seth of their dinner together last week at D'Angelo's.

He buzzed and was surprised when the front door clicked to grant him entrance. He climbed the four stories up to the number he'd taken note of on the directory, six, and waited a moment before raising his hand to knock.

But he never had the chance to do so, because Seth swung the door open. Dane would have liked to think it was eagerness that caused him to open the door before Dane had the chance to signal his arrival. But the smile planted on Seth's face told him otherwise— it looked panicked, terrified, a mockery of everything a smile was supposed to be.

"Hey," Seth said, his voice a trembling quake. "You made it."

Dane gave him a wary smile. "Yeah...." He moved to try and peer over Seth's shoulder into the apartment and was surprised when Seth took a step to the right to block that view.

"Listen, Dane, I'm really sorry, but something's come up. I'm gonna have to give you a rain check. The next pizza and the wine or beer is all on me!" He smiled hugely. Brightly. And falsely.

"What's going on?" Dane could feel his eyebrows moving toward each other in the center of his forehead.

"Nothing." That big fake smile again.

"Cut it out." Dane felt sick to his stomach. He had no idea what was going on, but all the signs were there to tell him he shouldn't like it. His happy mood evaporated.

Seth was beginning to close the door when another voice piped up from behind Dane.

"Yo! Someone left the door open downstairs. Pizza comin' through!"

Dane turned to see a slender young man with light brown hair and a few whiskers on his chin approach them. He wore a stocking cap and a fleece-lined denim jacket. He had a butterfly tattoo on his neck. His right hand held a large pizza box aloft. As he drew closer, Dane could smell the tomato sauce, the cheese, and the spices. It should have made his mouth water, but all it did was nauseate him. He felt even sicker when he looked back and saw that Seth had gone white.

Seth gave a sickly grin to the delivery guy.

"That'll be $26.50, dude." He took a breath, grinned, and said, "Before tip, of course."

"I'll be right back." Seth turned, closing the door behind him. But not all the way….

Dane knew it was wrong, disrespectful, and certainly none of his business, but he couldn't seem to help himself as he gave the door a gentle tap with his fingertips. He couldn't help it if the door swung open of its own accord.

He leaned in a bit to see into the apartment.

There, on the couch opposite the front door, sat a very handsome young man. He had a compact frame, but it looked bulked up and muscular. His dark hair was buzzed on the sides and longer on top, in a style Dane had heard the kids refer to as "high and tight." Dark eyes appraised Dane back. He wore a scoop-necked green T-shirt and

135

a pair of khaki-colored jogging pants. Nike high-tops were kicked off and lay, one up and one on its side, next to his long, stretched-out legs.

He looked very much at home.

Seth came back. He grinned at Dane, but it was one of the sickliest-looking grins Dane had ever borne witness to—ever. As Seth held out a twenty and a ten to the delivery guy, Dane noticed Seth's hands trembled.

"Thanks, dude. Enjoy your pie." The delivery person hurried off, and Dane watched him with a combination of longing and relief.

He turned back to Seth and cocked his head. "I know I have no right to ask—"

Seth held his free hand up to cut him off. "You do have a right. You were invited over here tonight, and it's only natural to wonder what the hell's going on." He jerked his head backward to indicate the guy on the couch. "I'm really sorry, but I had a completely unexpected person show up." He leaned in a little closer to Dane. "That's Luke. My ex."

Dane felt the bottom drop out of his stomach. "Oh," he said, his voice dry and husky.

"It's not like you think," Seth said.

"I didn't think anything!" Dane cried.

"Whatever. I just meant he was not invited here. You were."

"It's okay, Seth. He can come in. There's enough pizza to go around," Luke called from the couch. There was a touch of laughter, of mocking in his words, as though he not only caught the implications of the charged exchange between the two men in the doorway but was also amused by it.

Seth glanced over his shoulder, then back at Dane. If eyes could plead, his were doing just that. "I'm so sorry," he said. He reached out to touch Dane's shoulder. And without quite knowing why, Dane reared back.

"Yeah. I know. You told me. What do you want me to do?" Dane knew what he wanted Seth to do. *Throw the gorgeous hunk on the couch out and invite me in.*

Once that piece of business was accomplished, maybe they could sit down together and try to pick up the pieces and continue to move forward. He realized the rising symphony of emotions going on within him, making him feel both sick and enraged, could all be filed under *J* for jealousy. He wanted this Luke person out, right now, even though he knew he had no right to wish or hope for such a thing.

He was confused, though, by his jealousy. He couldn't remember the last time he'd felt that particular green-eyed emotion with such intensity.

"I think it might be better if you'd just go home tonight. Rain check?" Seth held the pizza box out to him. "Here. Take this home to your kids."

"And what will we eat?" Luke wondered loudly from the couch.

Seth rolled his eyes. He stepped out into the hallway and shut the door behind him. "Look. I don't want him here. I swear I didn't ask him here. If I had had any warning at all he was coming, I would have told him to stay in Chicago, where he belongs. He just showed up—unannounced—about fifteen minutes ago. He drove all the way from Chicago. I can't just send him away."

Dane wanted to whine "Why not? You invited me *first*." But he realized how childish it sounded before the words even got to his lips. "I understand," Dane said, even though he didn't. "What does this mean?"

"It doesn't mean anything." Seth shrugged. "It means circumstances beyond our control derailed our evening together." Seth leaned over and kissed Dane quickly on the lips. "I'll make it up to you, I swear. And again, this doesn't mean a thing."

Dane eyed Seth warily. "No? Someone drives, what, seven, eight hours just to see you and it doesn't mean anything? Don't BS me. At least give me that much credit."

"Seriously, Dane. I didn't ask him here. I don't want him here. I was looking forward—so much—to our evening together. But now that he's here, I have to deal with him."

Dane looked Seth up and down and, for the first time, noticed how good he looked. It heaped sadness onto his jealousy.

"I could wait," Dane offered. "There's the DanDee Bar just down the street. I'll go have a beer. You could call me when he's gone." Dane felt like his desperation showed. And he didn't care.

Seth shook his head. "I don't think that's a good idea." He pressed the pizza box more firmly into Dane's hands. "Take this home. Enjoy it with your kids. We'll talk tomorrow."

Dane looked down at the pizza box as though it were something else—he didn't know what. A concrete block, maybe, a piece of the sidewalk, a fallen star. He looked back up at Seth, wondering if the anguish he felt was obvious on his face. He felt sick to his stomach as the thought occurred to him that Luke might spend the night with Seth. Even if he stayed on the couch, the thought still made him want to be sick. "Okay. Sure," Dane said. What else could he say?

He turned away, expecting Seth to say "Oh, wait. What am I thinking? You can come in. Luke was just leaving," or words to that effect. Instead all he heard was the door close behind him.

He stared at the shut door for a long time, a hopeful little boy inside him waiting for it to reopen. When, after about five long minutes, it didn't, Dane walked away, head hung low.

SETH SAT on the opposite end of the couch from Luke, as far away as he could get. The two men had barely had a chance to talk when Dane arrived, when the pizza delivery showed up.

Luke nudged Seth with his foot. "Why'd you get rid of that pizza? It smelled good."

Seth glared at his ex. "What are you doing here?"

Luke held his hands up in a defenseless posture and gave him the smile that had once melted Seth's heart. "Hey! Is that how you treat a guy who drives seven and a half hours on a sometimes treacherous turnpike to see you?"

Seth settled back into the couch, letting his head loll back into the cushions. He pressed a hand to his eyes. "Yeah," he said. "You weren't just 'in the neighborhood,' so let's talk about why you're here."

The silence that stretched out after that was so long, Seth finally opened his eyes once more and turned a little, so that his back was against the arm of the couch and he was facing Luke. One thing he could never take away from the man was that he was a hunk, a hottie, a gorgeous specimen fit for the gods. But that's all he was. Seth had discovered, the hard and heartbreaking way, that Luke was an empty vessel, a pretty package with nothing inside.

"I came all this way," Luke said softly, his deep voice velvet, "to tell you how sorry I am that I fucked up. To tell you I still love you." He reached over and grabbed Seth's arm and squeezed it. "And I want you back."

Seth gave a bitter laugh. "You want me back? Really? After what we went through, after the way you hurt me?"

"Yes." Luke stood up and moved so he sat right next to Seth, their bodies aligned. He slid his arm around Seth's shoulders, pulling him close. "That guy was nothing to me. He was a mistake. That's all. I learn from my mistakes, sweetheart. It'll—"

"Never happen again," Seth finished for him.

Luke let out an abashed chuckle. "Yeah. I know, I know. That's what every cheater says, but I really mean it. I've been desperate for you since you've been gone. I've felt lost, unmoored. I can't eat. I can't sleep. The world's just not right without my Seth in it."

Even as Seth thought the lines were bullshit, a small part of him was hungry for them and ate them up. He hated himself for that.

When Luke moved that gorgeous face of his in for a kiss, Seth, as always, didn't know if he could resist. He lifted his face, parted his lips....

DANE TOSSED and turned. And then he turned and tossed. Then he angrily punched the pillows upright against the headboard of his bed and sat up, sighing. Through all the dark hours, he had tormented himself with thoughts of them together. He couldn't blame Seth for wanting to get back together with Luke. The guy was model material, worthy of a runway or some photo shoot for a men's fitness magazine. He was hot with a capital *H*.

Dane visualized them in all sorts of positions. Positions he had gleaned from all the porn he had surreptitiously watched on his computer over the years. There was Seth on his back, his legs on Luke's rippling shoulders. Here was Luke on *his* back, holding his giant, glistening cock up so Seth could slide down on it. There they were, in a sixty-nine. Doggie style. Reverse cowboy.

Each variation taunted and sickened Dane, making the very idea of sleep impossible.

At last, sitting up, legs apart, staring into the pitch darkness of the room, he was able to force his mind away from the mental pornographic loop playing endlessly and question why he was feeling such jealousy.

He hadn't really allowed himself to think it until tonight, until life and its endless and often cruel surprises forced the realization out into the open.

You're in love with Seth.

There. He'd thought it. In so many words.

And his timing was impeccable. Just when he realized he could, and did, love another man, that love was usurped by someone who looked like Joe Manganiello and Christopher Meloni had a baby and it grew up to be Luke.

What chance did oversized, dowdy Dane have against a stud like Luke?

None! Get serious.

His mind returned to the fantasies that made him want to vomit. In this one, Luke's come was spurting all over Seth's face and Seth was hungrily trying to catch some of the copious white with his tongue.

In spite of himself, Dane got hard and stared down with horror at the erection that had sprung up in his boxers.

Just then his phone, next to him on the nightstand and silenced for the night, made the *brr* noise that indicated an incoming call. It moved a little across the smooth wood surface as it vibrated.

"Who the hell?" Dane wondered, hoping and wishing. He picked up the phone and saw two things simultaneously: Seth was calling, and it was a little after 2:00 a.m.

He accepted the call. "What?"

"You awake?"

"No, sound asleep. What are you doing?"

"Come over? Please."

It had been a long time since Dane had heard words that made him so happy. He suddenly felt invigorated, like a teenager again. "I'll be right there."

He leaped from the bed and began gathering up his jeans and T-shirt from the floor where he'd left them in despair, not even three hours ago.

SETH REMEMBERED Luke moving in for that kiss. He recalled how freighted with promise that kiss was, and he knew, without consciously thinking it, that if he opened his mouth and let Luke's tongue in, he was doing more than just kissing the man; he was letting him back into his life.

And that he could not do.

He recoiled, leaning back from Luke, and shouted, "No!"

"No?" Luke's astonishment said he seldom heard the word, especially from a gay man he was about to kiss.

"No." Seth pushed him away and forced himself to stand, even though his knees felt so weak he worried they wouldn't support him. But his knees, and his resolve, were both fine—and strong.

"You gotta get out of here."

"Baby, baby. What are you talking about? Sit down. Let's discuss this. I came all this way...." Luke gave him what Seth supposed he imagined was one of his most seductive looks.

"Yes, you did. And I didn't ask you to." Seth crossed the room, putting at least another six feet between them. "What you decide is not my problem." He pulled out one of his vinyl-covered chairs from the dinette set and sat down on it. Its hardness was a comfort. "Don't hold me responsible for what you decide to do on a whim. Contrary to popular belief, Luke, you're not as irresistible as you think."

Luke snorted.

Seth pondered for a long time before he allowed himself to speak the words on his mind. "But I do forgive you."

Luke's face, surprised, lit up in a genuine smile. "Really?"

Seth nodded. "Yeah."

"That's great." Luke patted the couch beside him. "Come back here." Soft. Seductive.

Seth would be lying if he said he wasn't tempted. Luke was so gorgeous it *was* hard to say no.

But Seth loved someone else.

And Luke needed to hear all he had to say, so he stayed rooted in his chair. "I forgive you, Luke. But I don't forgive you for *you*, I forgive you for *me*." He let his eyes meet Luke's, holding his gaze. He could see something dawn on Luke's face, something like understanding, and it made Seth a little sad. "I need to forgive you to let you go. A wise man once told me"—Seth smiled, and he hoped it conveyed kindness and not triumph—"that the opposite of love isn't hate. It's indifference." He did get up from the chair then and moved to sit on the couch with Luke, but not too close.

"I'm glad you made the trip, actually, because having you here, in this moment, allowed me to let go."

Luke tore his gaze away from Seth's and simply stared straight ahead, at the opposite wall. "Gee. I'm so glad I came. Glad I could help," Luke said.

And there's the man I'm lucky to be getting away from. Seth had felt a little guilty, a little saddened, but no more. He realized he'd always known, somewhere deep down, that while Luke had a big dick, his heart was tiny. He thought only of himself. And Luke's need to reunite? It was nothing more than ego driven, a balm to apply to his rejected soul. Seth recalled Luke telling him once, early in their relationship, that no one had ever broken up with him. "If anyone does the breaking up, it's always me." In retrospect Seth could see there was both a little pride in the statement and a warning. How dare Seth have the nerve to leave him!

There really wasn't a lot more to say. Finally, true to form, Luke asked a selfish question.

"Can I at least crash here tonight? I'm too beat to drive all the way back, and I'm too strapped to stay in a motel."

Seth could just imagine how Luke would use the quiet hours of the middle of the night to try to make some more moves on him, when he was most vulnerable. But Seth had other plans. He got up and went over to the kitchen counter, where he'd left his wallet after paying for the pizza. He rummaged inside and brought out three twenties. He pressed them into Luke's hands. "Summitville motels aren't nearly as expensive as Chicago's. This ought to get you a river view at the Vista, out on Route 7, just five minutes from here. My treat. Sleep well, and say hello to Chicago for me when you get back."

Luke looked down at the cash, then back at Seth. "You're a dick," he said softly.

"Okay. And now I need you to go."

They said nothing as Luke slunk from the apartment, slamming the door behind him.

And now he waited for the intercom to sound to tell him that his real lover had arrived.

He would answer the door naked.

DANE WAITED impatiently downstairs. He still clutched the bottle of Chianti in one hand, but he doubted very much they'd need it. He laughed out loud, the sound of it strange, floating on the deserted and silent downtown streets.

He felt like he was eighteen and told himself, *You know what this is? It's a booty call. An honest-to-God, middle-of-the-night booty call!* He laughed again, this time a little higher, maybe bordering just a tad on hysterical. He never imagined he'd find himself in such a situation, at least not now, not yet, not with someone he worked with.

But love and lust, Dane was learning, did not always work in tandem with that other L-word, logic. And thank God for that! He shifted his weight impatiently from one foot to the other as he waited for the click of the front door that would admit him to Seth's building.

And Seth's mouth, his lips, his dick.

His heart.

The click sounded, telling Dane the door was unlocked and he was free to enter. He placed one hand on the door, pulled it open partway, and stopped.

"Oh my God," he said aloud, just as a can skittered along on the sidewalk behind him, reminding him of what a ghost town Summitville became after midnight or so, maybe even earlier. "Oh my God, I have no experience. Not with a guy!" The titters came again, and this time they were hysterical. "I can't do this! I'll look like a fool. He's used to guys like Luke! Me? Are you kidding? He'll have to show me how to do everything, like some green boy. I'm not what he wants!" He said the words whispering, fast, and realized that if someone could overhear him, they would think he was completely off his rocker.

Dane contemplated just letting the door slam, fleeing into the night. He realized, much to his giddy horror, that when it came to gay sex, he was a virgin. A fucking virgin, in both the literal and colloquial senses. He couldn't go through with this.

The door clicked again, letting Dane know Seth was pressing his intercom entry button again and probably wondering why Dane wasn't at his door already.

You don't have to do anything you're not ready for, he thought. *You can just go in there and talk to the man. Get to know him better. Maybe a little touching, a kiss....* His dick rose in his pants a bit at this last thought, and that gave him the courage to enter the building and mount the stairs. His little internal pep talk sounded like something he'd say to one of his students or, God forbid, his kids. And *that* thought made his dick wilt a little.

Still, he continued up the stairs.

Seth waited at the door for him. He wasn't wearing a stitch. Dane couldn't help it. The dizzy laughter rose up in him like a horde of bees, undeniable, and he doubled over, barely able to catch his breath.

Seth stepped back. "Well," he said nervously. "That wasn't quite the reaction I'd hoped for." He stepped back a little farther and slid the door open a little wider. "I guess I need to get myself to the gym. Pronto."

"No, no." Dane held his hand up, trying to rein in the laughter and catch his breath. Tears poured down his cheeks. He was laughing so hard he wondered if it could lead to something cataclysmic, like a heart attack. "It's not that. You're beautiful. Perfect." He managed to choke the words out between breaths, between dying bursts of laughter.

He paused at the doorway, face-to-face with Seth. "You still want me to come in?"

"Of course. Get in here."

Dane stepped inside, and Seth closed the door behind him. Even in the soft glow of candles Seth had set up around the room, Dane could see that Seth's face was beet red. Seth hurried away, presumably into his bedroom, and returned moments later wearing a white terry-cloth bathrobe. He snatched the bottle of wine from Dane's hand.

"What gives, man?"

Dane could detect a note of anger in Seth's voice. He didn't blame him. What man wants hysterical laughter as the response to his naked body?

Dane made for the couch, grateful to be able to sit down. He allowed himself a few moments to just sit and breathe—in and out—before responding. At last he patted the couch next to him. "Sit down, sit down. Open that wine if you want."

"I think we both need it. School night or not." Seth disappeared into the kitchen. Dane heard a door open and close, the *pop* of the cork being removed from the bottle, and then the *glug-glug-glug* of glasses being filled.

He returned, sat down next to Dane, and handed him a glass. He didn't toast, and under the circumstances, Dane thought that was entirely appropriate. He took a gulp of the red and was grateful for its warmth and immediate calming influence.

"Look, Seth, I'm sorry I laughed. It wasn't at you."

"What was it, then?" Seth snapped. "*With* me?"

"No! No, of course not. You don't understand." Dane fixed him with an expression that he hoped conveyed not only his sorrow but also his confusion and despair. Dane put it baldly. "I'm just scared. My nerves got the better of me."

"Scared?"

"Yes! Yes, I've never, I've never, I've never…." His voice trailed off. Now, instead of laughter, he feared crying. No, he wouldn't let himself.

"You've never what?" A light bulb popped on above Seth's head, and his lips turned up in a small smile. "Never been with a man?" he finished.

Dane shook his head and gulped down the rest of his wine. He leaned forward to refill his glass.

"I just thought—" Seth started to say.

Dane finished for him. "That I what? Had secret experiences behind my wife's back? Or maybe, to give me some credit, played around a bit before I settled down and got married? Is that what you thought?"

"Well, yeah. I can't imagine having an attraction like ours and never acting on it, especially when you're in your twenties."

"Katy and I got married when we were just out of college. Even in high school, we were the school's 'it' couple all through school, from freshman year on. We lost our virginity to each other when we were both fifteen. It was fun. Hell, when you're that age, any sex is fun." Dane shrugged. "We always had an okay sex life, but toward the end, I thought more and more about men, and sometimes, in order to follow through, you know, I needed to fantasize."

"That she was a man?"

"God, no!" Dane chuckled. "Katy was too much of a woman for that. And it wouldn't have felt right for me. I would have felt like I was cheating." He shrugged. "I imagined I was this hot straight guy."

He peered into Seth's eyes, Seth supposed, for understanding.

"It worked for me."

"So you never, ever acted on it? Back when I was first coming out, I used to cruise some of the lakefront parks in Chicago, and half the guys I hooked up with were married. I guess I just assumed you did something like that. Sorry for making assumptions."

"No. No, it's not an unreasonable thing to think. I even know there's a rest area out on Route 7 where guys meet up to exchange blowjobs." Dane snorted. "Some folks around here refer to it as 'Lollipop Park.' I can't say I wasn't tempted to check it out once or twice… or more. But I could never go through with it. My family always meant too much. I mean, what if I got caught, got arrested? A high school teacher? In this little burg? Can you imagine?"

Seth leaned forward and touched Dane's knee, which sent something akin to an electric jolt through him. "I can't, Dane, I really can't. Most of my life has been spent out of the closet. I never even really had a girlfriend, not a serious one, anyway."

"So you never...?"

"What? Had sex with a woman? God, no. And I can't imagine that either, nor would I want to try." Seth gave a mock shiver. "I don't even know if I could."

"Now, now. It's not that bad." Dane drank some more wine, a little slower this time. It was relaxing him, or maybe it was finally opening up to someone about who he really was that was doing the relaxing. "I just realized, when you called me up in the middle of the night and asked me over, that it would be for more than hot chocolate and cookies."

"What kind of cookies?" Seth wondered. "Because I do have some Chips Ahoy in the kitchen."

"Shut up." Dane punched Seth in the arm.

"Ouch." Seth rubbed at his shoulder.

"I got really nervous. I *am* really nervous." Dane searched Seth's eyes for a glimmer of understanding. He was relieved to find some there, along with a measure of kindness.

Seth took one of Dane's hands and held it fast. Dane could never have imagined that holding hands could be so sexy. The heat, the smoothness of Seth's palm, were things Dane wanted to savor.

"You don't ever have to be nervous with me, Dane. We can go as fast or as slow as you like. You can leave right now, and we can try this again after some dating, or do you call it courting around here?" He snickered. "Seriously. We can take our time. Start off with a kiss, like this." And Seth leaned forward and very gently kissed Dane's lips, just letting his tongue flick the top lip for an instant at the very end. He leaned back. "Or we can go faster." His face morphed into an evil grin. "There's no pressure, is what I want to say. If, or when, we're together—and I do hope it's when—it should be about having fun, pleasure, being close. None of those things are stuff you should get uptight about.

"And in case you're wondering, I am totally cool with your virginity. I'm a teacher, for crying out loud." He grinned. "So I won't mind showing you the way. Making you do it over and over again until I'm sure you have it right." He touched Dane's face. "You're such a beautiful man. You know something?"

Dane wasn't able to speak, so he just shook his head.

"The moment I saw you, in the school parking lot, on my first day, I was a goner. I hate to sound all mushy and everything, but I think I fell for you in that moment… with the snow coming down all around you." He sighed a little. "Just this gentle giant that seemed not only in command of himself but also, somehow, enormously kind and compassionate." Seth drew in a breath and then said, "And so, so sexy."

He leaned in and kissed Dane again, this time for longer. Dane allowed his tongue to slip between his lips, and Dane kissed back. The stubble on Seth's face, curious and strange after years of only feeling Katy's smooth skin against his own, was powerful and intoxicating.

Dane had no words. He leaned back into the couch, letting the taste of Seth, his kiss, linger on his lips with his eyes closed. He wanted him to do it again. And again. Forever.

But another part of him told him that now would be a good time to go home. It had to be getting close to dawn, and he didn't want to be gone when Clarissa and Joey awoke. He and Seth had opened a door tonight, and he felt that portal had given them entrance to many rooms, which would take a long time to explore.

Dane surprised himself by saying, "Maybe we could just go in your bedroom and lie down for a bit?"

Seth grinned at him. "Just lie down? For a bit?"

Dane nodded. "Baby steps."

"Okay, tiger. I'm buying what you're selling." Seth stood and tugged Dane up by his hand. He led him into his bedroom, blowing out all but two candles as they headed toward the threshold. He let go of Dane's hand and lifted the two votive candles, letting their flickering light lead them both into the dark bedroom.

They stopped next to the bed. Dane could feel his heart, its beat staccato, pounding against his chest. He sucked in some air when Seth let his robe drop to the floor and stood before him, strong, erect, naked. Dane tried to swallow and found it difficult.

148

"Wow," Dane murmured.

"We're just gonna lie down," Seth said, and did so.

Dane struggled out of his own clothes and lay down beside him, Seth's naked body a silken thing next to him, a gift. He drank him in, like a man who hasn't had a meal in ages: the furry chest, the line of hair that led down to his cock and balls, his strong, muscular legs. All of it had a sense of unreality about it. It was as though Dane had fantasized this image a million times and now was seeing it with not only his mind's eye, but also his real eyes. And for once, reality surpassed fantasy.

He gently let his hand, barely touching, glide across the fur of Seth's chest. "You're beautiful," he whispered.

"And so are you."

There was no need to ask for a kiss. They simply came together, one body, one desire, no more hesitation. Briefly, in their coupling and the igniting of their passion, Dane had a thought. *Why, there's really nothing to know here. I didn't need to worry. This is natural— just hang on for dear life and... enjoy.* But then even that thought was wiped away by the ecstasy and language of the lips and the tongue, the hands, and the dicks... which fit together so much better than Dane could have ever imagined.

Their passion, like a wave, rose as they hungrily consumed each other's mouth, then neck, working their way downward in synchronization until they both found they had the other's cock in his mouth. The taste of Seth's dick was so good, so natural, nothing odd... it was like coming home for Dane.

And he suspected Seth felt the same too, as he shot jet after jet of come into Dane's mouth, which he swallowed... hungrily.

After, they fell asleep for a bit, Dane's come and their warmth gluing them together and lulling them away.

The light filtering into the room was gray when Dane woke up. He kissed Seth's closed eyelids and sat up. "My kids. I have to get home. But we'll do this again. Soon." He grinned.

Seth mumbled sleepily, "Promise."

"Oh yes." Dane groped on the floor for his jeans. "Tonight?"

"Mmm-hmmm," Seth murmured. "And every night you're up for it."

Dane chuckled. "I'll be back." He leaned in, tenderly kissed Seth's lips, and then got up and headed to the front door.

And the most curious thing? He didn't feel the floor beneath his feet.

CHAPTER 16

DANE RETURNED home feeling like a kid again in so many ways. For one, dawn's pearlescent light was just creeping over the hills to the east, making the world around him appear in washed-out shades of gray. Yet there was a dull glow to everything, as if the world had been gilded. Or maybe that feeling of things being touched with gold was in Dane's head, a sort of afterglow. He smiled.

Sneaking home early in the morning like this made him feel like a teenager again. He recalled sneaking out of his bedroom window to meet up with the guys in the neighborhood to drink beer and other potables cadged from parents' liquor cabinets or refrigerators. It seemed so wild back then! If they were lucky, sometimes Buddy Rogers would manage to steal a fat and resinous bud from his brother Jake—who was a sophomore at Youngstown State University and kept a stash in his sock drawer—and he and his friends would get high, lolling around and giggling over the stupidest things. Until someone broke out the Twinkies and Doritos....

Dane, locking the car and heading up to his front door, recalled those days with nostalgia, but also a kind of perverse pain. Although he tried his best back then to hide it, especially from himself, he had an enormous crush on Buddy Rogers, who represented all the best parts of the good, solid German stock from which he was descended: dishwater blond hair, a cleft in his chin, and a body that was beefy, stocky, broad, but without an ounce of fat. Buddy was strength personified—with a goofy grin. Dane would try to make himself believe he and Buddy were simply best buds. *That* was how he rationalized the fierce sense of affection he had for him. It was hard to use that to explain away how he would find himself simply staring at Buddy as he took a bong hit or told yet another rude joke, but he made a good effort of it nonetheless. Only in Dane's adolescent dreams, he couldn't escape the fact that he was filled with desire for his friend. In those dreams there would be kissing, sucking, caresses of body parts that rarely saw the light of day. Dane would awaken from these dreams filled with guilt and shame, even though he would rationally ask himself, "Who has control over their dreams?" Often he would awaken with the inside of his boxers damp with come, which only served to make him feel more guilt ridden.

Dane could now allow himself to smile at the memory and how it segued into this very moment because once again, Dane found himself sneaking into his home after a night of debauchery.

Only the things he did with Seth through the long night? Those were not the stuff of dreams or a tortured imagination. They were real and too delicious to let the appearance of guilt or shame mar them.

Today also reminded him of mornings when he would slip back into his dorm at Miami University, on the other side of the state in Oxford, after spending the night with Katy in her dorm. He would feel somehow accomplished, and when his roommate, Jeff, would wake up to give him a sleepy yet knowing grin, Dane was proud. Proud to be part of the brotherhood of the straight. Wasn't that proof? Hadn't he passed the test?

He unlocked the door slowly and opened it the same way, praying the door wouldn't creak and that his kids would sleep through his reentry into the house. He had lingered much too long with Seth, and he knew it. But the kids, both of them, slept like long-haul truckers, and Dane usually would just about have to resort to beating on a saucepan with a wooden spoon to wake them.

Except for this morning.

Stepping into the entryway on what he thought of as silent cat feet, he immediately spied Clarissa, sitting with her arms folded and legs crossed on the family room couch. At the sound of his footfall, she whirled around and lasered a glare at him, eyes narrowed, lips pulled down into a frown.

Seeing her was so shocking and her expression so severe, it took Dane by complete surprise. So much so that he let loose a startled, nervous laugh.

"Oh, so you think it's funny?" Clarissa stood. She wore a nightgown Katy had bought her the previous Christmas. It was full-length, red plaid flannel, and when Clarissa had opened it, she'd made fun of it, saying something about "Grandma-style." But now she couldn't have looked less like a grandma. She looked like exactly what she was: his little girl, even though she was sixteen years old.

She put her hands on her hips and said the words disappointed mothers had been saying in similar situations for eternity. "Where have you been? I've been worried sick."

Dane simply shook his head and mumbled, "God."

"What?" Clarissa stared at him, her mouth slightly open. There was something like terror in her expression. "That's all you have to say? Are you going to tell me where you've been? I'm not used to my father sneaking in at dawn. And I shouldn't have to be."

And all at once, the joy Dane had felt after his night with Seth, a night that was truly a revelation, an awakening, a release in so many ways, evaporated. The evening and its joy withered in the face of his daughter's wrath and indignation.

He crossed in front of his daughter, swearing an icy chill emanated from her as he passed her and her unwavering stare. He kicked off his shoes and plopped down on the couch with a sigh.

"You gonna sit down here? So we can talk?" He reached for her hand, barely grazing the skin before she snatched it away. "Clarissa...," he pleaded. "Please."

She whirled on him, actually shaking a finger close to his face. It made him want to laugh. It made him want to cry. It made him want to yell at her and ask, "Who's the parent around here, anyway?"

She nudged him. "I want to know where you've been. I think I have a right to know."

And Dane felt the first inklings of an emotion he hadn't expected—indignation. Did she have a right? What were his rights? He breathed deep, trying to maintain some calmness, attempting to tell himself his daughter had been going through very rough times. Then he reminded himself that these were times in which he'd been available for her almost every nonworking minute of his life. And yet his almost constant availability and devotion were cast aside, as if they didn't matter. And what of all of Dane's heartfelt pleas for communication, for talking about things with her? Her reaction had been consistent, if nothing more. She would lock herself in her room, her head hunched over her laptop or phone. She'd whisk herself away down the street to her best friend Jerri Lynn's house, whose mom had mentioned to Dane that Clarissa was beginning to feel like a second daughter.

Dane peered into Clarissa's face for a few moments to see what he could discern, what he might read there besides anger. Her eyes were moist, red-rimmed. He realized she'd been crying. That hurt his heart and made him want to gather his little girl up in his arms, if she would let him—which he very much doubted.

"Well?"

Dane thought for a moment, thinking how what he would say next was important, that it mattered. He finally chose his path and knew she might not like what he was about to say. "Clarissa, I honestly don't know that where I was is any of your business. Parents, believe it or not, do have a right to some privacy."

"Oh, so you don't *want* to tell me. Never mind, Dad, you don't have to. You've always been great at keeping secrets, right?" She turned her wounded eyes away to stare out the window at their backyard.

"What do you mean?" Dane knew, and he bristled at the unfairness of her words. Or were they really unfair, or a justified reaction to his own lack of courage and self-acceptance through the years? Again he told himself to choose what he said and how he said it very carefully.

She didn't utter a word, a sound, for so long that Dane began to wonder if she was through talking to him—once again. Would she run off to her room? To Jerri Lynn's? Would he never reach her again?

Or maybe she wasn't saying anything because she somehow knew, knew exactly where he'd been and what he'd been up to? The thought caused a shiver to course through him.

But finally she spoke. "I wasn't born yesterday, Dad. I heard you leave in the middle of the night, watched your car back out of the driveway. You looked like you couldn't get out of here fast enough." She laughed bitterly. "You were with some guy, weren't you?" She shook her head.

Dane was a little relieved. At least the "some guy" reference gave him hope she didn't yet know which guy.

"How is it we go all these months barely speaking, and the one time, because yes, Clarissa, this is the one *and only* time I've ever left you and your brother on your own for a few hours, this is when you take notice? And not only take notice but are outraged?"

"So it's true?"

Dane debated whether or not to tell her. A lie was ready at his lips—someone from school, in trouble, needed him. He had spent the night with a sick or injured student at the emergency room at Summitville Hospital. It was credible, something Dane would do, and he took a small amount of pleasure in imagining the abashed look on Clarissa's face.

But that pleasure was small and mean. Her question was giving him an opportunity, and he recognized it. He said simply, "I was with someone I care about."

"A guy?"

"Yes. That does happen to be his gender. Is that important? Would you feel different if it was a woman?"

Clarissa shook her head, her lips pursing in a moue that could only be interpreted as disgust. "I guess not." She shrugged. "Who cares, anyway?"

Dane stood and put his arms around Clarissa, even though she didn't return the embrace, even though she, in fact, stood rigidly with her arms at her sides. Dane whispered in her ear, "I do. I care, honey. I'll always care."

She disengaged from him, just on the edge of pushing him away. "You have a funny way of showing it!" she shouted, and he could see the unshed tears standing in her eyes. "Abandoning us in the middle of the night. Shame on you."

Dane collapsed onto the couch once more. Clarissa might be on the brink of womanhood, but right now she was nothing more than a scared little girl, his little girl, in sore need of comfort. "Honey, won't you please sit down?"

Maybe because it was tiring to maintain such an air of righteous indignation, she did finally collapse on the opposite end of the couch. She stared straight ahead, rapidly twirling a lock of her hair and breathing faster.

"I did go out."

"Booty call," Clarissa whispered.

"Oh, come on, Clarissa. Grow up."

"I'm not the one sneaking out of the house like a thief. Don't tell *me* to grow up."

"I'll tell you what I want. I'm your father."

"Who was it?" She twirled her hair faster.

"Do you really want to know?"

She paused for a second, maybe considering. "No. It makes me sick." And then all at once she crumpled. She doubled over, and sobs racked her shoulders. Through her tears, she asked, "What would Mommy say? What would Mommy say?"

Dane scooted down the couch and put his arm around her shoulders, tentative at first, and when she didn't resist, he squeezed her to him. He realized, all at once, that Clarissa's confused feelings about him being gay were present, but the real root of her pain was the fear he'd replace her mother.

"Mom would say it's okay. Mom would want us to be happy. I know that."

She peered at him hatefully out of the corner of her eye. "How dare you."

Dane contemplated how to tell her what he was about to say and in the end, decided there was no other way than simply. "Clarissa, Mom has come to me."

Her tears ebbed a bit, and she looked at him again, curiosity usurping outrage. "What are you talking about?"

"In dreams. At first she wasn't accessible. She was turned away. But more and more, she began to show her face, and she told me that I'd be all right. We'd be okay." He sighed, closed his eyes at the memory, the memory of her. He felt his lips curl up in a smile and felt a warm rush of gratitude for those dreams and the opportunity— however ephemeral or brief—to be with Katy again. "I really think she's with us. She knows and understands," Dane said simply.

"Do you really believe that?" Clarissa asked with the sudden guilelessness of a child.

There's hope for you yet, baby girl.

"I do. I can feel her, all around us."

Clarissa returned her face to her palms and wept some more. Dane simply patted her shoulder, wondering if she'd cried like this since Katy's passing. Certainly not in his presence....

"Love doesn't go away because someone dies. What your mother felt for you, for Joey, and yes, even for me, is too powerful to just vanish. It's with us. It's always with us. You have to believe that, sweetheart."

Dane reached over, ever so gently, and removed Clarissa's hands from her face. He lifted her chin, forcing her to meet his eyes. He prayed his expression was open and kind.

"You have to believe that, because I see her now. In your face." Dane shook his head. "In you, I see the young girl I met way back when. You look so much like her, not just physically—" He grinned. "But buried beneath all that teenage angst is her light—her kind heart."

"I don't know how kind it would be if she knew about you. About your lies."

Dane closed his eyes and sucked in a breath. *Patience.* But Clarissa's words would have been no less painful had they been accompanied by a jab to the belly with a knife. "That's not fair, honey. The one person I lied to most was myself. But you know what *wasn't* a lie?"

Clarissa shook her head.

"This might surprise you, but what wasn't a lie was the love I felt, and still feel, for your mom. When it comes to love, real, pure love, we're not gay, we're not straight, hell, we're not even male or female. We're human. And I love that woman with all my heart. I always will.

"Sure, there are some things I've come to accept about myself since she passed away that change things. But it doesn't change my love for her, doesn't change the family we made—together.

"I don't know if your mother knew about me, my feelings, or not, but I do know that if she did, she would have taken it hard. But in the end, I truly believe she would have tried to understand and would have stood by me, because that's the kind of selfless person she was, and that's the kind of pure love we had.

"If she hadn't died that awful day last fall, you and I may have never had this conversation. I don't honestly know if I ever would have come out. Part of me was so scared to face who I really was. And the real terror was how much it would hurt the people I love.

"But things happen in life. And I saw, after the funeral, that there was no reason to keep who I was a secret anymore. I could be who I was, who I always was."

Was it possible? Did he see a softening in Clarissa's features? She licked her lips and stared at him with eyes that were mournful but not disdainful.

"Dad, oh Daddy," she whispered.

He touched her cheek gently with his fingertip. "Every time I look at you, Clarissa, I see her. In your grace, in your smile, in the way you relentlessly twirl your hair." He chuckled. "She lives on in you. She would be heartbroken if she knew we weren't living on as *family*. Because one thing I know for sure—family was the most important thing to her.

"And it is to me too."

Clarissa said, "So if I don't want you to be gay and I want you just to stay at home and be our daddy, you will be?"

Dane was taken aback by the question. "Honey?"

She smiled, and there was a hint of wickedness in it. "I'm kidding. I know you're a guy," she sighed. "And gay or not, guys have their needs."

Dane, a father, did not want to wonder from where such wisdom came, not when it emerged from the lips of his sixteen-year-old daughter. "I guess so, sweetheart. We all will have to make adjustments as we grow." *Like, for example, I will have to adjust to how you know about guys and their needs. Do we need to have another talk? Do I need to take you down to Planned Parenthood?*

"You okay?" Dane asked, because it seemed like there was little more left to say, at least in this moment. But for now it felt as though the door had swung open.

"I don't know." She smiled and reached for a lock of her hair and then jerked her hand away. "I guess so."

"You must be tired, sitting up all night. Worried sick."

She pushed him. "I was!"

"That makes me, in a perverse way, feel good. It shows you care."

"Daddy! I never stopped caring. I just didn't understand."

"I know. I know. And I know that we still have a lot of work ahead of us."

"So who's this guy?" Clarissa asked.

"All in good time. All in good time. You'll meet him." Dane prevented himself from adding "You already have." Saying that would only open a Pandora's box, and he didn't know if he was ready.

"Will I ever be ready for that?"

"Will I ever be ready to meet the man *you* love?" Dane wondered back.

"That's a *long* way off," Clarissa said.

"You never know, Clarissa. You never know. Love can sneak up on you when you least expect it."

There were other words they could say, more banter waiting in the wings, but for now they were quiet. And quiet was good.

At last, as a shaft of golden sunlight suddenly warmed the family room, Clarissa leaned over and hugged her dad. "I love you," she whispered. "Don't ever doubt it."

"I didn't—not really. And I love you too. With all my heart." He held her in his arms until they heard Joey stirring upstairs, the flush of the toilet, the tromp of his footfall at the top of the stairs.

They broke apart, but their smiles were warm.

MAY

CHAPTER 17

IT WAS one of those days with the promise of summer that always showed up in May. It gave people the false hope that summer had finally arrived.

Truman wasn't fooled. But it didn't change the fact he was going to take Odd Thomas out for a walk by the Ohio River and enjoy the dusk and the temperature hovering near eighty degrees.

He hadn't been down there in a long time, not since he'd told Patsy about the boy he used to meet there, along the pebbled shore. It was too painful of a reminder. But now that Truman was more confident in himself, he could let go of the pain and see that denying himself this small pleasure was only giving the boy power over him he didn't deserve. The boy hadn't earned it—or Truman's heart.

He and Odd wound their way down the bank overlooking the river, Odd leading the way through the barely there trail through the trees. They'd traveled this course many times together before, so much so that Truman often wondered if he and his dog had made this path.

He let Odd off his leash, and the dog forged ahead, racing down to the rocky river shoreline before Truman was even halfway there. The dog had an odd shape, befitting his name, but that sucker could *move*.

Truman hurried after him and, once at the bottom, with the clean yet slightly fishy tang of the river rising up to greet him, stood for a while just watching his four-legged buddy frolic at the river's edge. Odd tore back and forth, ears back, kicking up pebbles, then halting abruptly to sniff at some detritus that had washed up on shore—a piece of driftwood, a cardboard milk carton, cans, and even an old tire. On the last he lifted his leg, as if in contempt for littering.

But the garbage that managed to invade the shore couldn't take away from the river's beauty, and this spot—a special "secret garden" that belonged to him and Odd Thomas alone.

Truman made his way to the big log he liked to sit on, reminded by the ashes from a recent fire that he was not the only one to visit this particular part of the shoreline. But he knew he was one of the few, because he seldom encountered anyone else there.

Except for that one boy….

Truman wasn't so sure he wanted to think about him now, though. Not when a warm breeze, moving across the water, buffeted his body in a most delightful way, with its promise of summer. Not when he could look out at the brown-green flow of the river as it rushed by, in a hurry perhaps to make its date with the Mississippi. Not when Blue Point Island, just across from him, excited his imagination, tempting him, as it always did, to brave the current and swim to its shore. The island was small, tree covered, and completely uninhabited. It seemed to withhold secrets in its dark shadows and thick woods.

But Truman didn't dare get in the water. Those currents, in actuality, really weren't so lazy. They were fierce and had claimed more than one kid his age and younger. No, the river was like that boy—there he went again, thoughts drifting back to last fall, when they used to meet there—beautiful to admire from afar but deadly if you dared to attempt an embrace.

Truman leaned over and picked up a stick, tossed it for Odd to fetch. The dog gave out a single bark and tore after it. Tail wagging, he brought it back to Truman and dropped it at his feet.

"Ah, not enough of a challenge for you?" Truman stood, turned, and flung the stick toward the woods behind him. He didn't expect it to go too far, because he didn't have much faith in his ability to throw—he'd been told more times than he could count that he threw like a girl—but the stick, end over end, disappeared into the woods.

Odd rushed after it, kicking up sand behind him, with a high-pitched bark that was more like a scream. He disappeared into the woods, and Truman continued standing, waiting for him to come out.

It seemed to take longer than it should have. The light faded behind him, the setting sun staining the sky with golden light, interspersed with patches of electric blue and strands of cloud. The darkness and the shadows cast by the trees in the woods made him lose sight of Odd Thomas.

He began to worry, just a little. He'd heard tales of river rats the size of small dogs living around there. Maybe a horde had gotten hold of Odd.

Don't be ridiculous, Truman scoffed at himself. *He'll be back any second.*

And he was. But he wasn't alone.

Holding the stick in his hand, with Odd trotting beside him, looking up at him with damned adoring eyes, was the *boy*.

A smile, involuntarily, came to Truman's face, and he quickly shut it off. He tried to look as though he didn't care, but he felt like any second now he would begin shaking. He wanted to *believe* he didn't care but knew it for a lie.

"What are you doing here?" he asked. No one, Truman knew, would believe that the boy, his first sexual and love experience, was Kirk Samson, high school senior and quarterback of the football team. The same boy who'd tortured him countless times at school, verbally and physically.

Who would have thought this monster could sneak into Truman's life, stealing not only his body but also his heart?

"Nice greeting," Kirk said.

He threw the stick down the riverbank for Odd, and Truman sucked in a breath at the graceful power in Kirk's form. He was only seventeen but already had all the markings of a man—the broad shoulders, the muscles, the strong jawline and Roman nose. The wind lifted strands of his wheat-colored hair. Truman thought if he were directing a film of Kirk Samson in this moment, it would be in slow motion, with soft focus, while strains of violin music swelled.

The audience would be totally taken, totally charmed.

As was he? Truman didn't know. He'd spent the whole winter and most of the spring convincing himself he didn't care. He wanted to believe that his association with Kirk was toxic and that no good could come of it. Yet seeing him here tonight, in this place Truman once thought of as their own—their trysting spot—brought back the complicated and potent brew of desire, puppy love, and hopelessness he had felt when they were meeting up on a regular basis.

Kirk turned and smiled at him, which caused Truman, just like the books said, to feel a little weak in the knees. He strode toward Truman, and Truman couldn't help but notice how the faded and ripped jeans hugged his strong thighs, the way the Cleveland Browns T-shirt gripped his upper body, revealing its form and definition. But what caught Truman most were the boy's pale green eyes, like emeralds.

Truman gulped and wondered if he could manage an intelligible word.

"I hadn't seen you in such a long time," Kirk said. "And it was so warm out, I thought I might catch you down here."

Kirk's smile widened, and Truman could almost make himself believe it was sincere. Because the weak-in-the-knees feeling showed no signs of going away anytime soon, Truman plopped back down on the log.

"Isn't our timing excellent?" Kirk padded through the pebbles and river sand in his flip-flops and sat down next to Truman. The scent Kirk gave off was heady, a mix of grass clippings, soap, and something Truman couldn't quite identify but that was undeniably male.

Truman didn't, couldn't, say anything for a long time. But at last he found the answer to Kirk's question. "Our timing has always sucked."

"Oh, come on now, buddy. I was hoping we could let bygones be bygones. It's been a few months since we were alone together like this. Can't you just let it be…." Kirk shrugged and pointed to the span south of them, the bridge that connected Summitville to the northern panhandle of West Virginia. "Be water under the bridge?"

Truman had to laugh. "Water under the bridge, huh? Do you know what I went through because of you?"

Kirk scoffed. "Everybody at school knew. You were such a drama queen last winter."

"Oh my God. I can't believe you." Truman shook his head, slowly but surely coming to the life lesson that very ugly things could be wrapped in gorgeous packages.

"What?" Kirk asked innocently, smiling his megawatt grin again.

But this time the smile did not melt Truman's heart. It just looked desperate.

"What?" Truman repeated. "Yeah, everyone at school knew because of my drama queen antics, as you call them. And let me tell you, *buddy*, that this bitch is proud to wear that label."

Kirk leaned back and away from Truman just a bit.

"But you know what everyone *didn't* know?"

Kirk shook his head, but Truman could see the light of realization dawning in those incredible green eyes.

"Everyone didn't know that I attempted to kill myself because of *you*. Because you hurt me and made me feel worthless." Truman shook his head. "You used me and tossed me aside, like a piece of that garbage there." Truman pointed to a two-liter bottle of Diet Coke that had washed ashore, half filled with dirty water and river silt.

Kirk started to open his mouth to speak, but Truman halted him with an outstretched hand.

"Let me finish." He lowered his voice a notch, but not the intensity with which he spoke. "You know how many people I told about you? Not one. Not even my mother, and we're like this." Truman crossed two of his fingers to illustrate his point.

"Don't ask me why I protected you and your precious reputation. You certainly didn't deserve it."

Kirk leaned back even farther. In a voice that was a tad anxious and just a little breathless, he asked, "You're not thinking of telling anyone now, are you?" He peered into Truman's eyes. "Because you know, don't you, that not a fuckin' soul would believe you."

"Maybe not." Truman's face lit up, and he grinned. "But I wonder how many people know about that port-wine birthmark on your hip bone?"

Kirk gnawed his fingernails and spat something onto the ground. In a low voice, he said, "Anyone who's been in a locker room. It wouldn't prove a thing."

Truman shrugged. "Maybe not. But I think it might start some people thinking. Doubting. I mean, look at Mr. Bernard. He's all man, and *he* came out of the closet, even with having had a wife and two kids, and no one was really all that shocked." Truman stared off, trying to peer into the shadows the trees made on the island across the water. "Not everyone is a sissy like me. Not every gay person. Maybe you shouldn't be so afraid of who you are. People might not be as hard on you as you think. They certainly wouldn't be as hard on you as you were on me." And it was Truman's turn to stare pointedly.

Kirk didn't say anything for a while. When he spoke, though, he surprised Truman.

"Oh, you're so sure of yourself. But just because you think I might not understand you, don't get all high and mighty on me and think I don't know myself. Maybe I just don't know who I am yet." He glanced over at Truman. "You're lucky that way. You may have been the butt of jokes and got beat up on the playground a lot, but people always knew who you were. You had no choice but not to hide it. In a weird way, I envy you that."

Truman was shocked. He said softly, "Believe me, it's nothing to envy. Did you ever cry yourself to sleep because every kid in your class thought it was funny to call you a girl? Did you ever take an extra half hour to walk home from school so you could cut through the woods, hiding from those who would beat you up? Did you ever get down on your knees and pray to God to change you? To make you like everyone else? Did you ever wish just to be normal?" Truman stared at Kirk and saw no light of empathy or recognition dawn in his eyes.

"I didn't think so." Odd came bounding back, and Truman picked up the stick and flung it again. He wondered if the dog would ever reach an age where he would tire more easily.

Kirk leaned in close. "Look, I'm sorry your life has been hard. I just mean, you don't, I don't know, have to carry around a secret like I do. You don't have to wonder if no one would like you or want to be with you if they knew the truth of who you were. If they knew the kind of porn you looked at on the computer." Kirk snickered. "Or the shit that creeps into your dreams at night."

Truman patted Kirk's shoulder. "You'll be okay. Even if you come out. You know why? Because you're gorgeous. You're confident.

You're sexy. Coordinated. People will always be drawn to you. No matter what. You'll see. Someday you'll come out, and you'll have a bunch of gay friends and they'll all be just like you."

Truman picked up another stick, made lazy designs in the sand at his feet because he couldn't bear looking at Kirk. "Unlike me, who has to rely on being a 'free spirit,' or no, 'interesting' in order for people to take notice. Even if you came out, which you will eventually, you'll look down on me, you and your perfect gay friends. You'll still laugh."

"No. No we won't."

Kirk slid an arm around Truman, and Truman didn't know whether he should shrug it away or lean into the embrace. He was about equally divided, which put him in a tough spot for decision making. So he just sat there, listening.

"I'm not a good talker like you," Kirk said. "But I think what I'm trying to get at is you're a brave kid. You have the courage to be you."

"Did you read that somewhere? Have you been watching that TV show? *Becoming Us?*"

Kirk chuckled, "No. No, I mean it."

He leaned in, and before Truman could even ready himself, Kirk kissed him. It wasn't a friendly little kiss either, but a hungry one, with tongue and an almost ravenous intensity.

Truman couldn't pull away. Everything got blurry, got confused. And because he didn't pull away, the next thing he felt was Kirk taking his hand. For a moment Truman thought, *How sweet, he wants to hold my hand*, and then reality reared its ugly head as Kirk moved Truman's hand to his crotch. Truman felt Kirk's erection straining against the worn denim. And for a moment he considered doing what he knew Kirk wanted him to do, what he'd done so many times in the past. He could pull the dick free of its material confines, slip quickly to his knees, and take it into his mouth, sucking, swirling his tongue, teasing it until it spurted into his mouth.

There was temptation to do that again. If Truman really wanted it, could he call it being used? Weren't they both getting something out of it? His fingers pressed against the denim, and Kirk let out a small groan.

But then Truman remembered all those other times and all those other blowjobs. What happened after Kirk came in his mouth? Quick wiping up, sheepish grin, and vanishing into the woods.

Truman knew how the scene would go because it had been repeated so many times.

So he leaned back and disengaged his hand from Kirk's. "No. Not this time," he said, even though there was a pang of regret nagging at him.

"What do you mean?" Kirk asked, his words petulant, a little angry. He reached over quickly and gave Truman's crotch a little squeeze. Truman was equally hard; he knew it. Kirk said, "You know you want it."

Truman stood, and as if to show his allegiance, Odd Thomas came to sit quietly at his feet. "No, Kirk, I don't."

"Why not? C'mon…," Kirk urged.

Truman shook his head. "It would be just like the other times."

"No, it won't. I promise."

"You're just saying that because you need release. Go find it somewhere else."

Kirk's mouth dropped open. Truman realized he'd never refused him before. Had anyone had the nerve to refuse Kirk Samson? This must be a humbling experience for him.

"C'mon," Kirk continued to whine. "No one has to know."

"And that's just the problem." Truman took a step back, farther away from Kirk, and looked down on him. "No one ever has to know. You want to live a secret life when I've worked hard to make sure who I am is out in the open. I'm not ashamed. God made me who I am. He made you too. I'm not gonna hide anymore. What you do is up to you."

Kirk tugged the zipper of his pants down. Truman couldn't help but look.

"Please," Kirk begged. "Just once more. For old times' sake."

Truman shook his head. "You're pathetic. I gotta go." He started walking away. Odd was immediately on his feet and following.

"Why not, Truman?" Kirk called after him.

Truman paused at the entrance to the woods. He put his hands on his hips. "You know, you're just pretty enough that even I might

170

be tempted to make the same mistake again. Break my own heart again. Feel ashamed again." Truman paused, considered the budding trees above. Then he looked back at Kirk. "But I won't. And do you know why?"

Kirk shook his head.

"Because I got me a boyfriend, Kirk. And to be with you? Well, that would be cheating."

And Truman began the ascent up the riverbank without waiting to see if Kirk had a response.

CHAPTER 18

THE SUMMITVILLE High School gymnasium had been transformed. Thanks to yards and yards of white crepe paper, scores of silver Mylar balloons, and several strategically placed rented disco balls, the scene of basketball games and tortuous gym classes had become a portal to a magical wonderland. The decorating committee had arranged round tables around the perimeter of the dance floor. Each one boasted an arrangement of fresh ivy cut from senior Cathy White's parents' old redbrick home, which had an endless supply. Flickering fake candles topped each table.

The DJ was queuing up her playlists on the stage overlooking the scene of that year's prom. Right now, something soft and ethereal was playing.

Seth told Dane, "That's Helen Jane Long. I listen to her when I'm feeling meditative. Very new age. I'm surprised the DJ would choose that for a high school dance." He looked up at Dane in the pale, shimmering light and couldn't believe they were at the prom together. He wanted to laugh. He wanted to jump for joy. Of course, for all intents and purposes, the official line was that they were chaperoning the prom together. Dane was, after all, the designated senior class adviser, and Seth had led the decorating team, using money left over from the staging of *West Side Story* as that year's spring musical.

But here, in this moment, before they opened the doors to the prom-goers gathering outside the gym, expectant in their tuxedos and gowns, it was just the two of them and the pink- and spiky-haired DJ across the way, but she was paying them no mind.

"She's just messing around. Testing sound levels, I'm sure. She'd get booed off the stage if she tried to play that." Dane cocked his head and listened. "It *is* pretty, though."

"Wanna dance?" Seth leaned into him.

Dane laughed, abashed. "What? Now? Here?" Dane eyed the room nervously, as if a thousand spectators hid in its corners, in its shadows.

"Yes. Before anyone comes in. Before the place gets swamped with adolescent pheromones and chatter."

"What about the DJ?"

"She doesn't care. I think she's a lesbian, anyway."

Dane peered into Seth's eyes, and the ocular connection, as it always did, melted Seth in some places while hardening him in others. Dane touched Seth's cheek, and just the simple gesture caused a tingle to rush through Seth's entire body.

He loved this man! He couldn't help it. They had tried to be sensible, to not rush heedless into love, not when Dane was still nursing his family through the loss of Dane's wife and his kids' mother, not when Seth should have still been tending to his bruised and cheated-on heart.

But love didn't wait for the right time, as they both had learned. Love kept its own timetable, and how that schedule ran was a mystery. Secret trysts had gradually become more and more public—well, some parts of their relationship still remained *very* private. They did have some propriety, after all—until they were dating, in full view of not only the school but Dane's kids, who were surprisingly blasé about their father having a boyfriend.

Even Clarissa. Especially Clarissa. Seth knew it had taken her a while to adjust, but once she had, she embraced her father with passion and a fierce protectiveness. Seth would never want to cross her.

"So do you? For me?" Seth suddenly realized he desperately wanted this moment—just the two of them, alone, in the flickering light—in each other's arms.

"Well, maybe just a quick sweep around the dance floor."

They embraced—and began to move. As they stepped out and into open space, the DJ increased the sound of the music. Seth found himself melting into Dane's huge bear hug, his feet feeling as though they had left the floor. For a moment the room, the cheesy decorations, and even the music disappeared in the flickering light. For Seth, all that existed was this man, his warmth, his perfect fit as he embraced him. He laid his head against Dane's chest, listening to the rhythmic beat of his heart.

Seth thought of the slow fire of their relationship, how it gradually ignited and then leaped into flame, refusing to be denied. Over Dane's shoulder, he saw the DJ watching them, grinning.

The song ended all too soon, and Seth let Dane be the one to break away.

"We need to open the doors now."

"Let the hordes in." Dane nodded. "Can't we just barricade ourselves in here? Have our own private prom?"

Seth winked. "I'll give you your own private prom—later. At my place."

"We don't have to go there. Joey's staying at his buddy Ethan's tonight, and Clarissa will be here and then at the after-prom. She won't be home until morning."

"I like having you at my place," Seth said. "But are you actually saying we could spend the night at your house? In your bed?" They had made love at Dane's—when the kids were gone. Afternoon quickies on their lunch hours. Hurried mornings after the kids headed out to school. But never a whole night....

"I think it's time." Dane smiled. "And I think the kids will be okay tomorrow, facing you over pancakes and sausage."

"Well," Seth said, "as long as I don't have to cook them."

"Or better yet, maybe I'll take you to some seedy motel out on Route 7," Dane whispered in Seth's ear. "Make you my sex toy."

And Seth suddenly wanted to leave *right now*.

"Big words, big man." Seth started toward the bank of double doors opposite them. The noise from the crowd outside was a rising roar of voices and laughter. Seth glanced back at the DJ, who gave him a thumbs-up and launched into the theme for that year's prom, Paramore's "Ain't It Fun?".

As the music swelled, so did the crowds nearing the doors. Seth and Dane pushed them open and then stepped back, smiling and watching as a tsunami of teenagers entered the gym, smelling of perfume, cologne, hair spray, and most of all, hormones.

"Easy!" Seth cried. "No pushing!"

They flitted to tables, the more popular kids grabbing the ones immediately adjacent to the dance floor first, even though no one yet had the nerve to be the first to dance.

Seth eyed Dane across the heads of the crowd, smiling. Dane had worn a simple dark suit, and it made his shoulders look even more massive, while the dark color accentuated how trim the big man actually was. Seth hoped Dane appreciated the work that had gone into what he had on: a simple navy blue silk suit, white shirt, and blue-and-red-striped repp tie. He had tamed his curls with gel and left his glasses at home, putting in the contact lenses he seldom wore.

Tonight would be a first—spent at Dane's house. Seth hoped it would be the first of many.

IT WASN'T until much later, after everyone had settled at the various tables and the dancing had begun in earnest, that the last couple to make the dance entered the gymnasium.

Seth nodded to the double doors. "Just like him to wait to make an entrance."

He grinned, and Dane followed his gaze.

And there stood Truman, poised and waiting at the entrance to the gym. Seth felt his breath catch a little, having a quick vision of a scared boy who wanted to be invisible, atop a rooftop, ready to jump.

"Just like him," Dane said and chuckled. Dane gave a low whistle. "Look at that getup. Kid's got balls."

Truman, who was always at a loss for money, was never at a loss for imagination. And he was ever the richer for it. Tonight he wore black. A black sarong (probably a curtain, but who was analyzing?), black combat boots, and a cropped black jacket that Seth suspected belonged to his mother, Patsy. Under the jacket, a white T-shirt with one of Truman's sayings scrawled in marker across the front. Truman was too far away for him to decipher what the boy had chosen to highlight on *this* T-shirt.

And next to him stood Darrell Adams, an older boy from Truman's neighborhood, brother to Alicia, who was in the same grade with Truman and who had become his best friend, ever since she'd stood up for his sartorial choices in one of Dane's classes.

Seth leaned into Dane. "Looks like Truman is getting along very well with the Adams family."

Dane snickered. "The Adams family."

Seth shook his head. "Truman doesn't have bad taste. That kid is hot."

And Truman's date *was* hot. A couple of years older than Truman, Darrell Adams towered over him by at least a head. His skin was dark cocoa and stood out against the all-white tux he wore. There were no crazy embellishments on his suit, just the simple tuxedo, with a black cummerbund and bright orange silk tie, which matched the dyed strip in Truman's hair. The funny thing was, he was paying no mind to the crowd in the gym, who were slowly quieting as they noticed the couple standing poised, hand in hand, at the gym's entrance. No, Darrell only had eyes for Truman. He stared down at his date with something Seth thought approached wonder.

And Truman looked back up at him.

"If they don't both have stars in their eyes, I don't know what to think," Dane said. "I feel so proud of that kid."

Seth nodded as the newest couple to the prom moved forward. As if arranged, the dancers on the floor parted to make room for them. The song that was playing, some dance tune by Lady Gaga, halted abruptly. Seth looked over to see the spiky-haired DJ fiddling with her controls.

And an odd selection emerged from the speakers, from a band Seth was sure was popular when these kids weren't even born—the Flamingos. The song? "I Only Have Eyes for You." Darrell moved confidently to the center of the dance floor, as if the song, the dim lights, and the crowd stepping back to form a circle around the couple were all his and Truman's due. He stood and waited, hand extended, for Truman to follow. When Truman caught up, Darrell took him in his arms, and they swirled around the dance floor as everyone watched, smiling.

Seth shook his head to clear it of the fantasy. Actually only a few people noticed Truman and Darrell come in, but here was the thing—none of them seemed to care. Once upon a time, there would have been pointing and laughter, nudging. Name-calling. Even as recently as Seth's high school days, the thought of two boys attending prom together was unheard of, would have been an event to involve the school board and make the papers.

Seth looked around at the kids, more and more of whom had noticed Truman's arrival. Sure, there were a few smirks, a few rolls of the eyes, but nothing that appeared truly cruel or threatening.

"Things have come a long way," Dane said.

He took Seth's hand and squeezed it, intertwining their fingers. The gesture was not lost on Seth. Dane had never allowed them any kind of public display of affection, especially not at the school. Yet here was Dane, clutching his hand. Anyone could see. And Dane, clearly, was not afraid. Seth squeezed back and felt a lump form in his throat. Sometimes the smallest gestures could have the biggest impact.

Darrell and Truman actually waited by the doors until the DJ played the next song, which was a slow one, Beyoncé's "XO." Seth wanted to stand and applaud the DJ's choice. The song, with its lyrics about bright light even in the shadows, was a perfect metaphor for the young couple taking to the dance floor. He squeezed Dane's hand tighter as Truman and Darrell actually began to move together to the music—for real this time.

No, no one stepped aside to make room for them. That was fantasy. But reality was even better, Seth thought, because of all of the kids dancing right alongside Darrell and Truman. The pair—black, white, gay, gender flaunting—were just another couple on the dance floor.

And that was a beautiful thing to see.

And then Seth saw something that surprised him, maybe even made his heart ache a little. There in the corner, hardly discernible in the dim light, was the star quarterback of the football team, Kirk Samson. He looked handsome and masculine in his tuxedo, and his date, Amber Wells, stunning in a shimmering turquoise dress, her black hair in a messy upsweep that looked elegant nonetheless, clung to him, perhaps to try to get him to notice her.

Kirk stared at Truman and Darrell, clutching a glass of punch in his fist. Seth could read, even from across the dance floor, the longing and the envy on the young man's gorgeous face as he watched Truman and Darrell swirl together on the dance floor.

Seth didn't say anything to Dane, not yet. The moment was so clear, so sad, that Seth didn't think he could put anything about it into words. His gaydar had never picked up on Kirk Samson, but now it was dinging wildly, and Seth could see a hidden boy, unhappy and wishing for a different life.

Amber stood on tiptoes to whisper in Kirk's ear, and whatever she said made him laugh. But the laugh looked strained, his face tight. He clutched Amber to him, and she, mistaking his despair for affection, clung to him, laying her head on his chest. Over the top of her head, though, Kirk continued to watch Darrell and Truman dance.

"He wishes he could be them," Seth said to Dane.

"What? Who?"

And Seth nodded toward Kirk. "Can you see it?"

Dane didn't say anything for a long time, and at last, in a voice tinged with regret and pain, he said, "Oh yeah. I can see it, because that was once me."

"Once?"

"Yeah… and for a long time. Until you came along." Dane studied Seth's face for a moment, and then he said something that completely undid Seth. "Wanna dance?"

"You're kidding."

Dane shook his head. He stepped away from Seth a bit and held out his hand. "The time has come."

Seth took Dane's hand, allowing himself—in a little shock—to be led to the dance floor. There they did attract some notice as Dane took Seth into his arms and began moving gently with him in a little circle, shifting gracelessly from foot to foot. Seth chuckled a bit, but only on the inside. Dane was a terrible dancer. But here he was, in front of God, the school, and everyone, dancing with his man.

And no one said a word. No one cried out in disgust, or fury, or with recrimination.

They all simply danced.

And Seth made a point to let go of his fear of past hurts, of prejudices, and to feel the warmth of this man in his arms, trying desperately to dance, simply to please him.

He glanced over and saw Truman and could at last read the legend he had written across his T-shirt.

Seth smiled.

It said "One word frees us from pain: Love."

Seth stood on tiptoes to whisper in Dane's ear, "I love you."

And Dane looked down at him, smiling. "Ditto."

RICK R. REED is all about exploring the romantic entanglements of gay men in contemporary, realistic settings. While his stories often contain elements of suspense, mystery, and the paranormal, his focus ultimately returns to the power of love. He is the author of dozens of published novels, novellas, and short stories. He is a three-time EPIC eBook Award winner (for *Caregiver*, *Orientation*, and *The Blue Moon Cafe*). His novel, *Raining Men*, won the Rainbow Award for Best Contemporary General Fiction. Lambda Literary Review has called him, "a writer that doesn't disappoint." Rick lives in Seattle with his husband and a very spoiled Boston terrier. He is forever "at work on another novel."

Rick always enjoys hearing from readers and answers all e-mails personally. Contact Rick at:
E-mail: jimmyfels@gmail.com
Website: www.rickrreed.com
Blog: rickrreedreality.blogspot.com
Facebook: www.facebook.com/rickrreedbooks
Twitter: @RickRReed

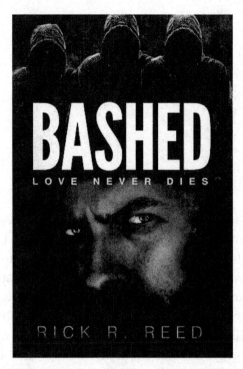

BASHED

LOVE NEVER DIES

RICK R. REED

It should have been a perfect night out. Instead, Mark and Donald collide with tragedy when they leave their favorite night spot. That dark October night, three gay-bashers emerge from the gloom, armed with slurs, fists, and an aluminum baseball bat.

The hate crime leaves Donald lost and alone, clinging to the memory of the only man he ever loved. He is haunted, both literally and figuratively, by Mark and what might have been. Trapped in a limbo offering no closure, Donald can't immediately accept the salvation his new neighbor, Walter, offers. Walter's kindness and patience are qualities his sixteen-year-old nephew, Justin, understands well. Walter provides the only sense of family the boy's ever known. But Justin holds a dark secret that threatens to tear Donald and Walter apart before their love even has a chance to blossom.

www.dreamspinnerpress.com

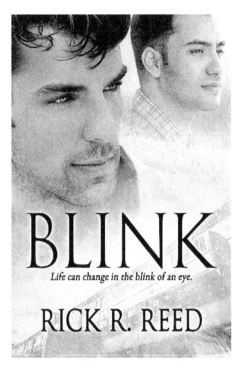

BLINK
Life can change in the blink of an eye.

RICK R. REED

Life can change in the blink of an eye. That's a truth Andy Slater learns as a young man in 1982, taking the Chicago 'L' to work every morning. Andy's life is laid out before him: a good job, marriage to his female college sweetheart, and the white picket fence existence he believes in. But when he sees Carlos Castillo for the first time, Carlos's dark eyes and Latin appeal mesmerize him. Fate continues to throw them together until the two finally agree to meet up. At Andy's apartment, the pent-up passion of both young men is ignited, but is snuffed out by an inopportune and poorly-timed phone call.

Flash forward to present day. Andy is alone, having married, divorced, and become the father of a gay son. He's comfortable but alone and has never forgotten the powerful pull of Carlos's gaze on the 'L' train. He vows to find him once more, hoping for a second chance. If life can change in the blink of an eye, what will the passage of thirty years do? To find out, Andy begins a search that might lead to heartache and disappointment or a love that will last forever....

www.dreamspinnerpress.com

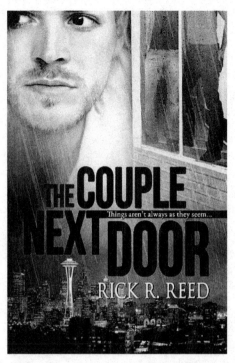

THE COUPLE NEXT DOOR

Things aren't always as they seem...

RICK R. REED

With the couple next door, nothing is as it seems.

Jeremy Booth leads a simple life, scraping by in the gay neighborhood of Seattle, never letting his lack of material things get him down. But the one thing he really wants—someone to love—seems elusive. Until the couple next door moves in and Jeremy sees the man of his dreams, Shane McCallister, pushed down the stairs by a brute named Cole.

Jeremy would never go after another man's boyfriend, so he reaches out to Shane in friendship while suppressing his feelings of attraction. But the feeling of something being off only begins with Cole being a hard-fisted bully—it ends with him seeming to be different people at different times. Some days, Cole is the mild-mannered John and then, one night in a bar, he's the sassy and vivacious drag queen Vera.

So how can Jeremy rescue the man of his dreams from a situation that seems to get crazier and more dangerous by the day? By getting close to the couple next door, Jeremy not only puts a potential love in jeopardy, but eventually his very life.

www.dreamspinnerpress.com

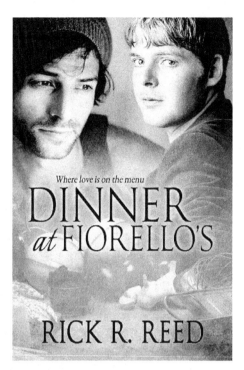

Where love is on the menu

DINNER
at FIORELLO'S

RICK R. REED

Henry Appleby has an appetite for life. As a recent high school graduate and the son of a wealthy family in one of Chicago's affluent North Shore suburbs, his life is laid out for him. Unfortunately, though, he's being forced to follow in the footsteps of his successful attorney father instead of living his dream of being a chef. When an opportunity comes his way to work in a real kitchen the summer after graduation, at a little Italian joint called Fiorello's, Henry jumps at the chance, putting his future in jeopardy.

Years ago, life was a plentiful buffet for Vito Carelli. But a tragic turn of events now keeps the young chef at Fiorello's quiet and secretive, preferring to let his amazing Italian peasant cuisine do his talking. When the two cooks meet over an open flame, sparks fly. Both need a taste of something more—something real, something true—to separate the good from the bad and find the love—and the hope—that just might be their salvation.

www.dreamspinnerpress.com

You never know where the love of your life might turn up.

When Matt Connelly suggests to his best buddy Cody Mook that they head to downtown Seattle to audition for the gay reality TV show *Husband Hunters*, both agree the experience might be a lark and a chance to grab their fifteen minutes of fame. What they don't know is that the show, modeled after HGTV's *House Hunters*, will open doors of longing neither expected. For Matt, the secret love he has long harbored for Cody might be thrust into the spotlight. Cody might realize his search for his perfect-forever-man extends no farther than the man who's always been at his side.

Husband Hunters promises laughter, tears, and, just maybe, a happy ever after. Will Cody and Matt's story be one of best-friends-to-lovers—or an outright disaster?

www.dreamspinnerpress.com

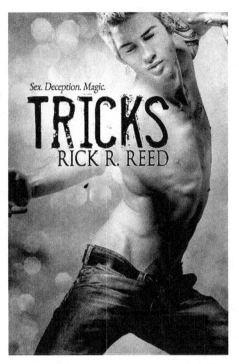

Sex. Deception. Magic.
TRICKS
RICK R. REED

Tricks can mean many things: sex partners, deceptions, even magic—or maybe all three.

Arliss is a gorgeous young dancer at Tricks, the hottest club in Chicago's Boystown. Sean is the classic nerd, out of place in Tricks, but nursing his wounds from a recent breakup. When the two spy each other, magic blooms.

But this opposites-attract tale does not run smooth. What happens when Arliss is approached by one of the biggest porn producers in the business? Can he make his dreams of stardom come true without throwing away the only real love he's ever known? This question might not even matter if the mysterious producers realize their dark intentions.

www.dreamspinnerpress.com

CPSIA information can be obtained
at www.ICGtesting.com
Printed in the USA
FSOW04n1022070916
24702FS